Murder at Christmas Manor

Mrs Capper's Casebook #6

David W Robinson

Prologue

Good afternoon and welcome to Christine Capper's Comings and Goings, your weekly video blog of what's been happening in Haxford, brought to you by Benny's Bargain Basement. For all your Christmas needs, whether so few or so many, you'll save time and money if you pay a call on Benny.

With the end of the year in sight, the beginning of December saw our full recovery from the ups and downs of the last twelve months. I say full recovery. In truth, Dennis was 99 % over the attack back in May. He still had some occasional speech difficulties, but that aside he was working full-time, five and six days a week, and rather than concentrating on administrative duties as he had been doing, he was under the bonnet, managing the spanners as he had always done.

The last month of the year was a time of reflection for me. The shocking attack on Dennis during the by-election, the struggles of his recovery, but more importantly, the dilemma I faced when dealing with the Leach business, made me question my career – I use the word in its loosest possible sense – as a private investigator. Was it time to give it up?

On the morning of Tuesday, December 6th, I

was due at the Radio Haxford studio for my weekly, Agony Aunt slot in the middle of Reggie Monk's morning show. Program director, Eric Reitman, rang me the previous evening and asked me to meet him in the market hall an hour before my slot was due, and even though I applied all the pressure I could, he refused to say what it was about.

With hindsight, I can tell you that it would be a turning point. Eric had not one but two surprises for me, and both of them were daunting to say the least. The second would drag me into the shocking events at Christmas Manor.

And one of the most curious things about the invitation was that when it came to the crunch, Dennis warned me about going. Was my husband turning psychic?

Let me take you back to the weeks before Christmas, a meeting in Haxford Market Hall, and a date with murder on the barren moors above Haxford.

Chapter One

Unless you were talking about cars, or more specifically engines, my other half was never the most perceptive or attentive of men. If, for instance, I stepped out of the house naked, carrying the day's rubbish for dumping in the wheelie bins, he would not say a word until I came back and then he would announce, "Those bags are heavy. I'd have dropped them in the bin on my way out to work." That I was wearing nothing but that which nature gave me would never register on his consciousness.

And yet, on the morning of December 6th, notwithstanding having heard me speaking to Eric Reitman on the phone the previous evening, Dennis broke the habit of a lifetime and asked why I was 'all dolled up'.

"I'll tell you later," I promised, and with a glance at the clock, told him, "If you don't get a move on, you're going to be late."

"Aye, well, in that case, I'll be late. Don't you think it's time we talked about us?"

His rhetorical question almost floored me, and I felt compelled to check that I really was wearing some kind of clothing. Obviously, I was. My dark business suit and white blouse if we want to be technical.

We talked about many things in our house, but I could never recall talking about 'us' and it compelled me to comment. "I didn't know there was anything to talk about when it comes to us."

"I'm not daft, Chrissy. I might be obsessed with motors, I might get a bit confused after the kicking I took in May, I might not have been the life and soul of the party for the last six months, but I'm not ruddy daft. It's Tuesday, and you do your agony aunt bit on the wireless on a Tuesday. No one can see you, so you don't get tarted up for that. I know how difficult things have been for you, but you've had summat on your mind since that last case you handled. The Leach geezer and his missus." He drew a deep breath, almost as if he felt hesitant about saying what had to come next. You could accuse my husband of many things, but never that he was nervous about saying what (he believed) had to be said. When he came out with it, I understood why. "I wouldn't blame you if you're thinking of calling us a draw, but we've been together nigh on thirty years and I don't want to see you go. I'm not gonna go all lovey-dovey on you. Us Haxford men don't do that kinda stuff. But I don't want to be without you. I don't know what I'd do without you, so I'm asking you, Chrissy, please think again."

Even though the absurdity of his conclusion tempted me to laugh out loud, I felt a sudden burst of love for this man. In all the years together, I was sure that this was the closest he'd ever come to telling me how much I really meant to him.

I bestowed a smile upon him that was just short of adoration. "Dennis, I'm not thinking of leaving you. I haven't had enough of you. Heaven knows, I should have, but I haven't. You are the most important thing in my life... after Bethany." I grinned to show I was only joking. "You are right, though. I have had something on my mind ever since I closed the Leach case, but it's absolutely nothing to do with me and you." This was the crunch. It was time to come clean on the torment I suffered during the Leach investigation and the stress of indecision it had caused me since. "The fact is I'm considering giving up my private eye's licence. Calling it a draw. It's partly to do with what happened to you and partly what happened with Gus and Petra Leach. As for getting dressed up this morning, if you'd been listening properly last night instead of watching repeats of Top Gear, you'd have known that the phone call was from Eric Reitman at Radio Haxford. He's asked me to meet him at Terry's in the market hall. He didn't say what it was about, but it's likely to be a formal business meeting."

"A formal business meeting? In Terry's Tea Bar?"

I glanced at the clock again. "Yes, and if I don't get a move on, I'll be late. And so will you."

***

Dennis's surprise at the location for my meeting spelled out its incongruity.

It wasn't often that I met with people in public. Most consultations and initial interviews and even research, whether as a private eye or a vlogger, took place in private, but with the Radio Haxford studio situated on the upper gallery of the market hall, whenever Eric and I met, it was at Terry's Tea Bar in the middle of the same market hall. We could talk in something approaching privacy and Terry did the best tea and toasted teacakes in Haxford.

Eric was the senior programme director at Radio Haxford, the man in charge of ensuring that the output went well. It was also part of his brief to come up with fresh ideas for the station, and it was thanks to him that my twice-weekly Lost Friends programme came into being. At one time Eric had suggested taking it to five programmes per week, but we scrapped that idea after less than a fortnight. Even so, where my fifteen-minute Agony Aunt slot went out live once a week in the middle of Reggie Monk's morning show, we recorded Lost Friends every Wednesday in the conservatory at my house, a job that took the better part of two to three hours. We worked that way because the studio didn't have much in the way of unused space, and our bungalow did. It wasn't an exclusive arrangement. Stella Briggs, the night anchor, put out her show from her attic… and no, I don't know how that worked other than she had an array of equipment hooked up to the studio.

At the outset, the money I earned from Lost Friends went some way to making up for Dennis's reduced income, and since we first aired in August, listener reaction had been excellent. Having started with the search for an old flame of my neighbour, Hazel McQuarrie, we had managed to reunite many people with friends they had lost touch with over the years. Since then, of course, Dennis had gone back to work full-time and my radio income, while not huge, helped us, even if only with the gas and electricity bills after the recent, scandalous increases in prices.

Eric was about fifty years of age, a well-educated man, who at one time in his life had been a director with a local BBC radio station. He was made redundant in a 'downsizing' operation which he rationalised as the Beeb farming out the contracts and looking for younger presenters to appeal to a younger audience. He was quite philosophical about the situation, and content to work for Radio Haxford where he had greater input into the output... if that makes sense. Indeed, the only thing about him which I could find fault with was that he employed his daughter, Olivia, as a gofer in the studio. Not that she was a bad girl. Quite the contrary. She was always amiable. It's just that she was thick as a brick.

Settling in at Terry's, with an hour to spare before I was due in the studio, we got the small talk out of the way and Eric went into his planned announcement.

Ever since he rang the previous evening, I had entertained the notion that he was getting ready to dump the two Lost Friends spots, and he would be trying to find a way of breaking it to me gently. It would be a pity, and I would miss the extra money it brought in, but I was ever the fatalist, and if that's what it came to, I would just have to deal with it.

He may have been hedging, but taking a leaf from Dennis's book, I did not beat about the bush. I asked him outright, and he hastened to put my mind at rest. "Agony Aunt and Lost Friends are great successes, even if we didn't run to five shows a week. Their appeal is down to your easy-going, local touch. You're a Haxford girl and the listeners love that, so no, we're not thinking of cancelling them. Exactly the opposite. Bearing in mind your success, we've had another idea. I just want to run it by you."

My interest began to rise. Especially when he described me as a Haxford '*girl*'. "Oh yes?"

"We talked about the Leach affair a while back. A nasty piece of work, Leach."

"His wife wasn't much better," I commented still wondering where Eric was going.

"It presented you with a bit of a dilemma, didn't it? The need to tell him the truth, and the concern for what he might do to his wife when he learned that truth."

"It did. As it happens, everything was reconciled, but yes, it did cost me some sleep."

He nodded judiciously. "And since then, according to your vlog, you're having second thoughts about your operation as a private investigator. Am I right?"

I hesitated. "It's a bit up in the air, Eric. Yes, I am considering my options. I mean, I've never made a fortune out of my work as a private eye, and as you know, it led directly to the assault on Dennis earlier in the year. Then I had this business with the Leaches, and... Well, I haven't quite made my mind up yet."

"Your vlog is quite successful, isn't it?"

The chop and change of subject had me slightly perplexed. I wished he would get to whatever it was he wanted.

In response to his question, I shrugged. "I do okay. I have a few sponsors. Doesn't pay me a fortune, but it's well supported." I toyed with my teacup and decided it was time to cut to the chase. "Forgive me, Eric, but could I ask you to get to the point?"

"Of course. How would you feel about turning your vlog fully professional?"

I was stunned into silence for a long moment. My vlog was already professional… if you counted a webcam and my laptop's editing suite to be professional. I did it all myself. I scripted it, recorded it, carried out minor editing work, posted it, and publicised it all by myself. I even drummed up the sponsors, people like Sandra's Snacky, Benny's Bargain Basement, Sonya's Unisex Salon, Pottle's Pet Supplies, and other local businesses. Obviously, if you were to compare it to one of the thousands of digital TV channels, there was no comparison, but for a small, home-based operation, I thought I did okay.

"I don't understand what you mean by turning it fully professional."

Eric sipped his tea. "It would be better described as a podcast than a vlog because it would be going out on radio not television. That would not mean you can't still record your videos and post to your site, but we would be asking you to record a more detailed version for Radio Haxford. The two might not even be the same subjects. I figure we could record our session in your conservatory along with your Lost Friends spots. The major difference is what we want as opposed to your vlog. Rather than the fifteen or twenty minutes you put out online every week, we'd be looking for at least forty-five minutes. That way, we can drop in the occasional commercial break and turn it into the full hour." He drew in a deep breath as if ready to make an announcement I would not find to my liking. "It would probably also mean definitely giving up your work as a private investigator."

I was going to interrupt but he hastened on before I could say a word.

"Not that there's anything principally wrong with you doing that kind of work while contracted to us, but if we were to go ahead, we would be looking for a serious commitment. You would have to ensure that you were available for recording every week, and for those times when you're planning a holiday, for example, you would need to record two or three episodes in a single session... or perhaps two sessions. We wouldn't want you floating off investigating this, that and the other for the world and its wife, leaving us hanging about to get the recording done."

I was both flattered and puzzled. "There's so much we need to talk about, Eric. I mean—"

"If you're worried about money, don't be. You'll be well recompensed."

"To be honest, I wasn't even thinking about money."

I can be quite skilled at lying when I put my mind to it. The moment he mentioned the idea, I had visions of lottery win type monies coming my way every quarter.

I brought my febrile thoughts under control. "I'm more concerned about the difficulty involved in turning a fifteen minute vlog into forty-five minutes. I mean, what am I supposed to talk about for three quarters of an hour? Barbara Timmins's attempts to stop the local cats using her garden as a lavatory and breeding ground, or the way the price of milk keeps going up in CutCost? Because that's the kind of routine stuff I put out on my vlog."

"First, the sessions will be properly scripted. Second, and in direct contrast to your weekly vlog, we were thinking more in terms of you spelling out your mysteries to our listeners." He held up his hands, and as he spoke, he spread them, as if spelling out a banner headline. "Christine Capper's Mystery Hour." He picked up his cup and drank as if he needed to lubricate his vocal cords. "We can line-up sponsors, and it will pay you very well, Christine. Not only that, you could find it's the launchpad to an entirely new career in broadcasting."

I wondered just how many more surprises I could take without prompting some kind of cardiac event. Still pondering the way he described me as a 'girl', I said, "I'm fifty-three years old, Eric. At my time of life, most people are thinking of early retirement not setting out on a whole new career."

He deployed his familiar patience. "You're a natural on the radio, Chrissy, When we first asked you to take over the Agony Aunt slot, it was Reggie who suggested you because he's been following your vlog since forever, and he knew how good you are. And if you recall, he was the one who interviewed you right here in Terry's Tea Bar. From the word go, you were a natural. You have a pleasant, smooth, even seductive voice. You're not boring, you don't put the listeners to sleep, and as I said, you're a Haxford lass. When we put Lost Friends to you, you were hesitant, but look how successful it's been. Our audience spikes when you're on. And don't give me this 'I'm too old' nonsense. Just to be personal, I suffered some health setbacks a few years ago. Nothing mega, but enough to remind me that I'm not getting any younger. I was overweight, eating all the wrong foods, drinking too much. I remember saying to my doctor, is it too late, and do you know what he told me?" Eric hurried on to answer his rhetorical question. "It's only too late when they nail your coffin lid down. Well, it's the same with you. You admitted to me a while ago that you had some financial problems with the attack on Dennis, on his subsequent, long-term sickness. I assume that now he's gone back to work, you're over them."

"And I told you at the time, Eric, that my financial affairs are none of your business. As it is, we're all right now that Dennis is back at work full-time. Considering the price of gas and electricity, any extra money is more than welcome, but for me to consider a career in broadcasting…? I'm not sure. I mean, I have no experience."

He chuckled again. "More nonsense. How long have you been running your vlog? Two, three years? Longer than that? And you should know by

14

now that speaking on radio is no different to speaking to your webcam. It's not as if you're appearing in front of a live audience." Eric toyed with his cup some more. "Let me tell you, Chrissy, the decision on the programme has been all but confirmed. If you don't do it, we'll find someone else, and they'll probably be talking on mysteries from all over the world. You have a huge advantage. All the problems, puzzles, cases you've come across are here in the Haxford area. A Haxforder talking about mysteries in Haxford to a Haxford audience. If that's not a winner, I don't know what is. It's the chance of a lifetime. Say yes, and I guarantee that the deal will be rubberstamped before the end of the year."

That would be some doing considering there were only twenty five days of the year left.

I was tempted to agree there and then, but I reined in my gut reaction. "No. I don't mean, no, I'm not interested, I mean, no, I need to give this some thought. How long do I have?"

He lapsed into thought, and when he spoke again, it was in tones that would brook no argument. "There is another item I have to mention, Chrissy. We've been invited to send a team to Christmas Manor on the twenty-second. Christmas can be a time of great loneliness for some people. We'd like to broadcast your Lost Friends from there. It won't cost you anything, obviously. You get two nights in a top-flight hotel, slap up meals, and we'll stand the booze bill."

Eric reached into his pocket and took out a large photograph of the place, which he smoothed out on the table.

I was expecting a regency manor house or something of that nature, but in fact, it looked like a small clutch of stone-built farm buildings, with one part set at right angles to the other, and a sort of redbrick annexe added on at the rear.

"You can't see it from this photograph, but Lyle Noelle, the new owner, has built a huge extension at the rear where the dining room, ballroom and guests rooms are located on three floors."

Right away I realised that it would interfere with my Christmas shopping and one of the highlights of my year was Christmas shopping. Dennis hated it. True, he hated shopping of any description he even considered the weekly visit to CutCost to be 'shopping' and I've told him hundreds of times that there's a difference between the 'weekly shop' and 'shopping'. The one is a necessity, the other is a pleasure. While he doesn't disagree on the former sentiment, he is quite clear on the latter. Pleasure is stripping and rebuilding an old engine. Shopping is anathema and he reserves most of his loathing for Christmas shopping.

Still and all, I found Eric's proposition appealing but with a slight reservation. "Considering the amount I don't drink, it's not going to cost you much." I cast a pointed stare at him. "Is this conditional upon me accepting Christine Capper's Mystery Hour?"

He shook his head. "Nothing of the kind. I just said, it'll be Lost Friends. That's on the twenty-second. Sixteen days from now. I'll give you until, let's say, twentieth to think about Christine

Capper's Mystery Hour, by which time I'll have to have a decision from you." He smiled. "And you know exactly what decision I want."

Chapter Two

Dennis gaped as I concluded the tale over breakfast the following morning. "You're gonna be a star on the wireless?"

I spent much of the previous evening mulling the pros and cons of Eric's offer, so much so that I skipped an old episode of Midsomer Murders, an even older episode of Dalziel & Pascoe, and eventually left the digital channels to Dennis and his repeats of Top Gear and Bangers & Cash.

He never questioned me, even though sixteen hours previously, he had entertained doubts about my confidence in our marriage. With breakfast upon us, and the Radio Haxford crew due at lunchtime, I decided it was time to tell him what had happened the previous day.

To say that he was elated would be an understatement. Wolfing down a mouthful of cornflakes, he grinned. "Hey, will I get free plugs for Haxford Fixers?"

I answered with a disapproving frown. I had been working for the station since May, and although he made the occasional effort at disguising his voice while ringing during my Agony Aunt phone-in sessions, I had warned the call handlers not to put him through. Radio Haxford was not in the business of giving free advertisements to the presenters' partner's business ventures, and anyway, even with the cost of living crisis, or perhaps because of it, Dennis and his partners had more than enough work to keep them in bread and jam.

I made an effort to curb his enthusiasm. "I don't know so much about a star, Dennis, but Eric was definite about one thing. It will be a commitment, and it will mean giving up my work as a private eye."

My husband grinned. "Then why are you dithering? Face it, lass, your private investigations haven't done you many favours, have they? All right, so you made a few bob, but look at what they've cost us. I ended up in dry dock because of one of them. Yes, and the clown who had me beaten up, threatened you first, didn't he? And only yesterday morning you were moaning about the problems you had with Gus Leach. And then there was that writer woman who lived up on the moors. Anita Stockings or whatever she was called. I mean, that other private eye tried to get your knickers off when you were working for her, didn't he?"

I dismissed most of his argument. "I made good money on some of those cases, Dennis."

"Yes, you did, but I'm back at work full-time, and it's not like we're desperate for the cash anymore, is it? And if this radio program turns out as good as yon Reitman reckons, you'll probably earn a blinking sight more." The look of doubt crossed his features. "Unless he's trying to get your knickers off, too."

I laughed. "You make it sound as if Nathan succeeded in getting my drawers off and he didn't. If that's what Eric is trying, he's wasting his time. You know me better than that. Anyway, he's a happily married man and his daughter works at the radio station. No, Dennis, he's not trying to seduce me. He's trying to make Radio Haxford a success, and at the same time, turn me into a success."

Dennis dug into his pockets, came out with this phone. "In that case, give him a bell, tell him you're up for it."

I shook my head. "The decision is not that simple. Right now, I'm mistress of my own destiny, so I intend giving it a serious coat of thinking about first."

He hid his disappointment behind a shrug. "Just make sure you're the mistress of your density and not mistress of your producer."

"Destiny, not density," I murmured as he made ready to leave for work.

***

Aside from the occasional reminders that he needed a decision by the twentieth, Eric barely mentioned the mystery hour during the next two weeks. He did, however, ask me for a written account of the Graveyard Poisoner episode from the previous Christmas, but when I asked why, he gave me what amounted to a skimpy explanation.

"It's for our script department. I need to see whether they can generate a decent, forty-five minute programme from your notes."

The term 'script department' almost made me smile. The entire department consisted of a word processor operator named Jill Bleaker. She used to work for an accountant. That was before he got caught offering shady deals designed to hide his clients' money from the taxman, whereupon he got four years and Jill got a visit to the job centre followed by a place at Radio Haxford. In between typing formal letters and memos from the station to listeners and staff, she turned out scripts for several programmes, including Lost Friends. She wasn't bad. Not exactly Hollywood material, but she did have to pen the cues for the music which I and other presenters had to read out. Everything had to get past Eric's critical eye, naturally, but her work was adequate for a local radio station.

A chubby woman, fifty-six years of age, she was true to her name. After speaking to her, a number of people could be heard to say, 'the outlook is bleaker' and with the best will in the world, she was a diehard prophet of doom.

"You're going to Christmas Manor on the twenty-second?" she said to me a couple of days after Eric had mooted the proposition. "Rather you than me. You know how easy it is to get snowed in up there, and the forecast is not good you know."

I responded by telling her that meteorology, weather forecasting was not a precise science, and long-range forecasts were often hopelessly wide of the mark. Jill was not persuaded.

"They've been saying for months, Christine, that this winter will be the worst we've had for years."

While unrepentant at delegating the task of

writing the script to Jill, Eric remained cautious. "Christine Capper's Mystery Hour is a bit more complicated than Lost Friends or Stella Briggs's Small Hours show," he said to me, "and we need to be sure Jill can cope. If there's any doubt, I'll get Olivia to give her a hand."

That was not calculated to inspire confidence. Olivia was Eric's dateless daughter and with her helping to write the scripts I would have to watch for her billing it as *'Crappy Christie's Mysterious Hour'*.

If I decided to take it on.

It was a decision I hovered over for most of the two weeks he had granted me, and during that time, if Eric didn't badger me, Dennis had no hesitation. He nagged the pants off me practically every day, constantly urging me to drop my private eye licence, and sign on for Radio Haxford's Mystery Hour.

"Christine Capper's Mystery Hour," I corrected him.

"There you go then. You'll be famous and making millions of pounds a year." He laughed. "What will you do about the begging letters?"

"Get you to stop writing them."

On the face of it, it didn't seem like a tough decision to make, and if I said I wasn't tempted, I'd be lying. Recording Lost Friends was hard work, but it amounted to a few hours a week. Totally different to my Agony Aunt spot which, for all that it was only fifteen minutes long, took only one hour a week: a half-hour briefing, mainly to advise me on the subjects to avoid, fifteen minutes to deliver the slot, and a fifteen minute debrief. All up then, Radio Haxford took up no more than three or four hours of my time every week. If we took on recording a mystery hour, it would expand to perhaps eight hours a week, and even though Eric hadn't talked money, I knew that the week's combined effort would pay me anything up to three hundred pounds, possibly more.

My work as a private investigator paid an average of forty to fifty pounds per hour, but cases were rare. I'm fond of saying that Haxford is not the largest town in West Yorkshire, as a result of which, it's not exactly a hotbed of crime, adultery, or missing persons – the three categories of case I usually took on. In a good year, I would take on half a dozen cases. Most of the time, it was three or four clients per year.

Some simple arithmetic would underscore the advantages of working for Radio Haxford.

But it wasn't all about money. The actual recording process, coupled to Lost Friends, would eat up one day, but what about the background work, the research, the necessity of drafting an account of one of my 'mysteries' so that Jill (and please, God, not Olivia) could produce a script? That would involve at least one more day, possibly more.

I also had to consider Dennis's glee at the prospect of my 'fame'. I was already quite well known in Haxford, but I didn't have charities badgering me for personal appearances. Reggie Monk was beleaguered with them, and he spent a good deal of his free time turning out for church fetes, WI meetings, Darby and Joan club shindigs, and so on.

On the other side of the coin, he got the occasional call to open shops, clubs, indoor sports venues, and the like, and he didn't do those for free. Whisper had it that he charged anything up to £1,000 a time, and when he was opening nightclubs, he availed himself of as much free drink as he could safely scrounge. Working as a private eye, the best I ever achieved was a free cup of tea when I interviewed clients in their homes/offices.

Finally, as I said to Dennis on the day after my initial meeting with Eric, there was the commitment. I was beholden to no one other than the one day of recording and an hour playing agony aunt. If I chose to take a few days off, I didn't need to ask permission. If I went ahead with the mystery hour, I would lose that freedom. On the other hand, I did have something like a thousand regular vlog viewers and if I didn't post every Thursday, questions were invariably asked on social media.

Overall then, it was a much more complex decision than simply saying, 'sod it, I'll chuck my PI licence away and become a radio personality.'

Even so, common sense prevailed, and largely on the back of Dennis's nagging, I finally made my decision on the evening of the nineteenth, and on the morning of Tuesday the twentieth, I arranged to meet Eric at Terry's an hour before I was due in the studio to deliver my Agony Aunt spot and the moment we sat down, I told him I was happy to go ahead with Christine Capper's Mystery Hour.

I guessed he was prepared for me by the way he

brought his briefcase along. He never had in the past. When I made my announcement, he cleared a space on the table, opened the briefcase and took out a contract.

I had signed one for Lost Friends so I was quite familiar with it, but Eric insisted on going through the major clauses, and as he did so, I switched off and wondered just how he would have reacted if I had turned him down.

When it came to recompense, I told him I was more than happy with the fees, which were on the order I had expected, but he was at pains to stress the thinking behind them.

"We can't pay the same as we pay, say, Reggie, or Stella. They're on air five days or nights a week, and both have a great deal more experience than you. But make a go of this, Chrissy, and a year or two from now, you could be on parity with them."

I wasn't altogether sure I wanted parity with Reggie Monk. I'd seen the wreck of a car he drove. In fact, Dennis did the servicing and repair work on it. But being famous in two years was a fairy tale fantasy for me…well, famous in Haxford, and not just for being married to the best mechanic in the business (Dennis's modest opinion, not always mine).

The contract was for a minimum term of two years when it would be subject to renewal/renegotiation.

"You can bring an agent in at that point if you like, Chrissy, but it's not guaranteed to get you a bigger slice of the pie. It didn't do Reggie, or Stella any favours."

I gave him my most self-assured smile. "I was a cop, remember, and then a private eye. I'm perfectly capable of haggling on my own, thank you." I borrowed his pen, signed the contract with a flourish, spelled out my name in capital letters, and dated it. There. Now I was committed.

"We'll get a copy to you, ASAP," he told me and tucked the contract back in his briefcase. "Now, about Thursday and Christmas Manor—"

"Oh, I meant to ask about that," I interrupted. "Does this hotel have a private room where we can record Lost Friends?"

His disarming smile should have warned me, but it didn't. For a brief instant, I thought he really was going to make an effort at seducing me as Dennis had suggested. He would, of course, be wasting his time. Other peoples' adultery had caused me enough agony to last a lifetime: Eileen McCrudden and Petra Leach to name but two. And they were only clients... well, Eileen was. Petra was the subject of an investigation, the adulterer not the adulteree... is there such a word?

As I said to Dennis, however, Eric was a married man and as far as I could judge devoted to his wife and daughter. In the case of the latter, he had to be. Without his watchful eye on her, she was perfectly capable of shutting down not just Radio Haxford but the actual town of Haxford.

Naturally, Eric was not about to make any obscene or salacious suggestions, but that would depend on your definition of salacious. His announcement was surprising, certainly, and from my point of view it was outrageous, bordering on

26

scandalous.

"We will be delivering Lost Friends from Christmas Manor, yes, but we'll also be delivering the first of Christine Capper's Mystery Hours, and both times, it will be broadcast live while you're in front of an audience."

A shock like that could kill, I decided. It didn't kill me though. Obviously, or I wouldn't be here to tell you all about it, would I? I believe it came close, though. My heart leapt and I was sure it tried to get out of my chest. I felt as if there was something like the alien in, er, *Alien*, trying to burst its way out. When it settled back into place it was pounding. When I tried to lift my cup, take some calming refreshment on board, I found my hands shaking so badly that the tea spilled from the cup. Quite an achievement considering it was already half empty.

"No," I said when I finally found my voice. "No way can I perform in front of a live audience."

"Christine—"

"It's so far out of my comfort zones, Eric, that it's in Blackpool… and just so we both know what we're talking about, I don't like Blackpool."

"Chrissy—"

"I can't do it. It will be a disaster. I mean, recording for the radio is one thing. When I make a mistake, you just go again, and you of all people should know how many mistakes I make. Do that in front of a live audience, I'll end up looking a complete idiot, just like…" I almost said, 'your daughter' but I caught myself just in time, and finished lamely, "that politician who told us we can

27

cut down our gas and electricity bills by living on sandwiches and soft drinks. I'm sorry. I can't do it."

He waited a moment to see if I had any more to say. When I didn't he went into one of his motivational pitches. "Everyone has to face it at some time, Chrissy. And you won't come away looking a complete idiot, trust me. The script is written. Jill's done a superb job. You'll have it in front of you on a tablet, and all you have to do is sit there and read it, just as you do in your conservatory when you're recording Lost Friends. Focus on the screen, forget the audience are there, and just read as you normally do. And just to put you right, you don't make many mistakes. A fraction of those made by Reggie. He doesn't stop to worry about it. He just laughs it off."

"Because he has more experience than me. He's glibber." I frowned. "Should that be more glib? Glibbier?"

Eric laughed. "You see. You can drop the odd quip in which would bring the audience down on your side."

He was trying his best to encourage me, but I wasn't having it. "Hardly... er..." I struggled to think of a comedian who knew how to handle hecklers. "...Hardly Billy Connolly, is it?"

He laughed again. "Radio Haxford couldn't afford Billy Connolly."

He could see that his attempt to lighten the mood did not work. He reached across the table and took my hand, which, according to my memory, was about the most intimate he had ever been with me, and I wasn't sure I liked it. Still, I resisted the

28

urge to pull away while he went on.

"Christine Capper," he began, almost as if he was going to tell me he was hopelessly in love with me, "I've been in this business all my life and I've seen many a young man and woman as nervous as you. A few never made it. Most did. You fall into the latter group. You are a natural for radio and for live performance. Even if it is only in Haxford. Trust me on this. It will be the making of you."

This time, I did pull my hand away. "All right, Eric. But bear in mind that if it's a total catastrophe, you're to blame."

Chapter Three

I was up with Dennis on the morning of the 22nd, and he was surprised to find me getting ready for departure to Christmas Manor.

"You're leaving me on me own for two days? You could have told me about it," he moaned.

"I did tell you. Two weeks ago when Eric Reitman first arranged it."

"Reitman? Again? He's after taking you to bed."

I almost replied, 'well, it's time somebody did' but I stopped myself. "Difficult. His wife and daughter will be with us."

Having failed in his arguments so far, he shot a dour eye through the kitchen window taking in the grim, heavy cloud above the town, then brought his attention back to me. His lips pursed in a scowl of disdain, he swept a hand over the lock screen of his phone, called up the browser, and opened the weather page of the previous night's Haxford Recorder. "You do know that they're forecasting blizzards?"

"What was it you once said to me?" I put on a face pretending to strain my memory when in fact, I'd already prepared my rejoinder. "The Recorder couldn't forecast the service date of a Triumph Herald, even if they have a full service record in front of them. Your words, love, not mine."

The speed at which he replied, he must have been ready for me, too. "I was talking about the ruddy sports pages when I said that. This is the weather, and it's not just the Recorder saying there'll be blizzards. It's the same all over the telly. They reckon this is gonna be one of the worst winters on record, and it's due today."

I recalled Jill Bleaker telling me much the same thing a week or two back. "Yes, Dennis, I know, but—"

He cut me off. "No, listen, Chrissy. I know Haxmoor. It's one of the furthest places from any town in the country, and if I had a fiver for every time I've had to go out in winter and tow some clown back who's got stuck in the snow, I'd be able to take the day off. And if it's really bad, like it was back in – when was it – about ninety-two-ish, even I won't be able to get up there with the wrecker. And if it comes down too heavy, the ploughs won't be able to cope. They'll have to wait until the snow stops. I'm telling you, Chrissy, you could end up trapped up there."

I reached across the table and took his hand. "It's not like I'm living in a tent, Dennis. And it's not as if I'm on my own. We have a full team going up there, and there are about sixty invited guests. It's a hotel, not a rundown birdwatcher's hide."

"Oh yes? And suppose you don't get back in time for Crimmy? You're the one who likes the parties, seeing Simon, Nam, and Beth—"

"Naomi and Bethany," I interrupted to correct him.

31

"Nam likes to be called Nam, and her and Simon both call Bethany, Beth."

Another angle occurred to me. "The arrangements are made, Dennis. Are you sure you won't be missing me? Are you sure that's not what you're worried about?"

"Don't be daft. We were apart for weeks when I was in dry dock earlier this year. I didn't miss you then."

"Mainly because you were unconscious most of the time." Time, I decided, to get hard. "I repeat, the arrangements have all been made, you knew about it a fortnight ago, or you would have if you were listening to me instead of the TV. It's too late for me to back out. I will be away for the next two nights and I'll be back on Christmas Eve."

"If the snow's as bad as they reckon, you could be there until Valentine's Night."

Determined to end the argument, I glanced at the wall clock. "It's twenty-five past seven. Don't you think it's time you were getting off to work?"

He got to his feet. "Suit yourself, but don't blame me if you get stuck out in the middle of Haxmoor for three weeks." And with that, he left.

Anyone listening in might assume that Dennis was simply being selfish, that he wanted me here to cook his meals, tidy up after him, and so on, but after three decades together, I knew my husband slightly better. He was genuinely concerned for me, and to be honest, if I had a choice in the matter, Haxmoor was the last place I'd visit on December 22nd, especially with the threat of heavy snow moving in, but I'd agreed a fortnight earlier and notwithstanding Eric's bombshell of live audiences, I didn't have a choice.

Haxford itself sat in a deep valley, surrounded by hills and moors, and as Dennis declared, Haxmoor was the most remote. Twelve hundred feet above sea level, there were only a couple of narrow roads crossing from Haxford to somewhere in the Longendale area, right on the borders of West Yorkshire, Greater Manchester, and North Derbyshire. It was spartan country, one of the most inhospitable areas of the region, and there had long been some suspicion of the nineteenth century builders' questionable sanity in putting up a grand manor house so far from civilisation. I say builders when what I really mean is the gormless fool who commissioned the building. Lord Noelle, a man whose wealth rivalled that of the famed Barncroft family. If the Barncrofts owned most of Haxford town and the immediate surrounding area, old Noelle owned most of the surroundings moors and charged local farmers for grazing their sheep on his land. This despite the fact that most of them were tenant farmers. In other words, they didn't own their land, Noelle did, and they didn't own their farms, Noelle did. They just paid rent, and more usurious charges for letting the sheep graze on what these days would be classed as common land.

Over the years, the manor fell into a state of disrepair, and eventually came into Haxford Borough Council's ownership. Less than a year ago, they sold it back to one of Lord Noelle's descendants, Lyle Noelle, a man who had made his millions doing whatever it was he did. Something in the City, so we all understood. I never did learn what happened to the title. He certainly didn't tout himself as Lord Noelle, but whatever his ancestry, he claimed to have spent a fortune on the place, bringing it up to twenty-first century snuff, and was now on the point of opening it as a hotel, and finally, he had renamed it Christmas Manor.

The grand opening was planned for Christmas Eve and guests would be paying a small fortune for three days and nights of absolute, luxurious decadence. Speaking personally, it would have to be heaven upon earth before I would fork out over £1,000 for three nights in an eighteenth century manor house, but that's me; Yorkshire through and through.

Prior to the grand opening, Noelle had invited about sixty guests, all of whom would be staying free of charge, and amongst them was our small team from Radio Haxford.

When Eric first invited me, I was both flattered and surprised. My Lost Friends spots were good and they had plugged the forthcoming Christine Capper's Mystery Hour for all they were worth over the last couple of days, but I still wasn't convinced that my popularity warranted such an august invitation, especially when I learned I would be performing live.

Eric hastened to reassure me yet again. "Christine, since you joined us earlier this year, you have proven yourself one of our most relaxed, pleasant, fluent, and popular broadcasters. Lyle Noelle is seeking cheap, even free publicity, and we're obliging. Reggie will be putting on the disco every night, Noelle has invited other entertainers, most notably a soprano named Diana Delancey, an opera singer, and there's a masked ball scheduled for one evening. Delivering Lost Friends and one of your mysteries to the audience, you will shine. And don't forget, both are going out live on Radio Haxford at the same time."

That still filled me with dread and I told Eric as much.

"Everyone in radio has had to go through this, Chrissy, and you'll be fine. Honestly. Hell, you could even make it into television."

And that brought on another panic attack.

If there was nothing to stop me going to Christmas Manor, there were domestic issues to sort out. As Dennis hinted, Christmas was a family time, and traditionally, Simon, his wife Naomi, and their daughter Bethany, the absolute light of my life, would come to our place for Christmas lunch. Our daughter, Ingrid usually managed to pay us a visit in the run-up to the festive season, but as a professional club singer based in Scarborough, she was usually on duty over the entire yuletide period.

The most important considerations were Dennis and our pet feline, Cappy the Cat. Our neighbour, Hazel McQuarrie, agreed to look after our moody moggie, so it was only a case of sorting out Dennis's meals. I couldn't leave it to him. There was only one word to describe Dennis Capper In the kitchen: *lethal*. Breakfast and lunch were no problem. He would take both at Sandra's Snacky in the mill where he and his business partners had their premises, and for his evening meal, we arranged that he would go to Simon's where Naomi would ensure he was properly fed.

Beyond that, the only thing I was left to organise was clothing. I could hardly sit in front of an audience of invited guests wearing a pair of jeans and a T-shirt which declared 'I luv Blondie'. So, much to Dennis's irritation, on Tuesday afternoon, I took myself off to Leeds, the nearest city which could be described as anything like cosmopolitan, and spent a sizeable wedge of money on a gown and other accoutrements, including a collection of paste jewellery which would gleam in the ballroom lighting at Christmas Manor, thereby convincing the audience that I was as well off as them. I also picked up a pair of shoes at a price which Dennis insisted he hadn't paid for his last three pairs of working boots. I accepted his observation. He tended to buy his footwear from a cheap stall on Haxford market, but as I told him, I could hardly sit before these people wearing a fashionable gown and jewellery, enhanced by a pair of steel toe-capped safety boots.

Thus prepared, my suitcase packed, the time coming up to 8 a.m. on a grim, December, Monday morning, I was waiting only for the Radio Haxford team arriving in the people carrier, and the great adventure would begin.

I wasn't sure what time the guests would arrive at the manor – probably in their fancy cars – but we needed to be there early so that the engineers could set up the equipment, and all the incomprehensible, technical gubbins so the sound balances, acoustics etc. could be dealt with before the festivities got under way.

Right on cue, at quarter past eight, Eric Reitman rang me, informing me that the minibus was leaving the town centre and would be there to pick me up in ten minutes, and with his customary punctilious approach to everything, he was spot-on time.

There were less than a dozen of us, so I was surprised to learn that it was twenty-seat bus, and behind it was a large trailer which the driver, Oscar Iveson, manoeuvred up the street in reverse. I wasn't sure I could do that with my car never mind a bus with a trailer behind it.

"All our equipment and personal luggage is in the trailer, Chrissy," Reggie Monk told me as he took my case while I locked up. The cold weather made his body odour almost tolerable, but even so, I decided I would not sit alongside him on the bus.

I popped next door to leave Hazel a set of keys to the house and accepting her best wishes and an assurance that she would be listening in for my live broadcast(s), I climbed aboard the bus, looked around, spotted an empty seat across the aisle from Eric, and sat down.

"When you're ready, Oscar," Eric called out. "Christmas Manor here we come."

The bus pulled away and as we turned towards Haxford centre, Eric indicated the woman alongside him. "Christine, allow me to introduce my wife, Beryl. Beryl, this is Christine Capper."

It was too far for us to shake hands, so we just smiled and mouthed 'pleased to meet you'. At least, that's what I was saying. I've never been the world's best at lip-reading, so for all I know, she

37

might have said, 'So you're the old bat my husband reckons is the best thing since sliced bread.' I don't think so. I think it was 'hello' but it could just as easily have been something less complimentary.

I'm not really intimidated by people, but Beryl lived up to the thoroughly middle class image of her university and BBC educated husband. Where I was wearing my jeans, Blondie T-shirt, thick jumper and quilted coat, with a pair of sensible, fur-lined winter boots on my feet, she wore a pair of plain, black pants, a dark top beneath a dark grey cardigan, and flat shoes. Her coat, which looked to me like a full-length wool job in a lively green, was on the rack above them.

She was some kind of senior teacher in a comprehensive school or sixth form academy, and from the set of her brunette perm and minimal make up, allowing a view of only the tiniest creases around her eyes, I guessed her to be Eric's age… about fifty, and that immediately called into question her heritage. She was a year or three younger than me, so what on earth possessed her parents to name her Beryl? The only answer I could come up with was wealth.

I had an Aunt Beryl on my mother's side, but she died when I was about six, and she was born sometime around the turn of the century… nineteenth to twentieth centuries, I hasten to add. Well, it's difficult to see how she could have been my aunt if she was born around the Millennium, isn't it? The logical conclusion of this pointless train of thought was that no working class family of the 1970s would name their daughter Beryl. I could see Bonnie after Bonnie Tyler, perhaps Britt after Britt Eckland (or the Britt version of Pippa doll) but Beryl? Any poor girl would be torn to metaphorical shreds in the schoolyard for a name like Beryl. So when I thought about it, when I applied private detective-ish logic to it, I decided Beryl Reitman was born to money.

Given Eric's income, I suppose the same could be said of their daughter, Olivia, whom I noticed sat towards the back of the bus with our new sound man, Tim Farrell. She was a pleasant enough young woman, but sadly, thick as a two long planks, never mind short ones. For months after I first began work for Radio Haxford, she persisted in calling me Copper and she often described me as Copper the Copper (I used to be a police officer). The message finally sunk in but only after I developed the habit of calling her Oliver. Unlike her parents, she had never benefitted from a university education. To be honest, I don't think she benefitted from her secondary education. Her listening skills certainly demanded some attention, for which reason I'd always refused tea or coffee when she came round with the studio's wish list of a morning. I was worried about ending up with a brandy and skimmed milk, or worse, a T&T – tea and tonic.

As for Tim, well he was a good few years older than Olivia, a nice enough and highly skilled man when it came to sound and acoustics. Tall, average looking, more hair around his bearded face than he had at the crown. He'd only been with Radio Haxford two months, but to judge from the way he was cosying up to Olivia, he hadn't wasted any time getting his feet under the Reitman family table.

There were a few other people on the bus, none of whom I knew by name, but recognised from the Radio Haxford studio and my conservatory on recording days. Technicians, gofers, and the like.

With the bus on the move, worming its way through Haxford, looking for Haxmoor Lane which would take us on the steep climb out of the town to the moor and manor, a thought occurred to me.

"Eric, why has this man renamed the place Christmas Manor?"

"Vanity, I think. I don't know Lyle that well, but as I understand it, he decided that a suitable play on his name would be Christmas. Remember the French for 'merry Christmas'? *Joyeux Noël.*" Eric pronounced it with an almost perfect French accent which reminded me of Francois Ketchak – real name Frank Kilsby – whom I met during the Wool Fair case. Not that Kilsby spoke anything like perfect French. More like euro-gobbledygook, but he pretended he was French when I first met him.

Eric was still talking. "He was going to call it the Noelle Manor Hotel, but thought of Christmas and there you have it. The Christmas Manor Hotel. He thinks it'll go down well with potential guests, especially at this time of year."

"Hmm." I had my doubts. "He could well end up with a barren time at Easter though."

Chapter Four

We were barely three quarters of the way through the climb to the Haxmoor plateau when the snow started to come down with serious intent, and that prompted our driver to begin grumbling from behind the wheel.

"Be lucky to get there at this rate, boss," he said to Eric.

"We have every confidence in you, Oscar."

Eric might have had every confidence in our driver, but I didn't share it. Not that I had anything against Oscar. After watching him reverse the bus and trailer up Bracken Close without actually hitting anything, I was sure of his top notch transportation skills, but the bus was beginning to slip and slide as it struggled up the hill and our speed was down to something like 10 or 15 mph. Either side of us, the steep walls of moorland grasses were already turning from autumn scrub to winter white, and Dennis's warning rang in my head. If it was this bad here, what would it be like another couple of hundred feet higher up when we levelled out on the moor?

We didn't have long to wait before we found out. I guessed that no more than another five minutes passed before we finally made level ground, and it was an almost total whiteout. Snow, driven by fierce gales, lashed at the windscreen, and even on high speed, as fast as Oscar's wipers could travel through their arc, the glass was covered again. His headlights blazed away and reflected from the blizzard just a few yards ahead of us. He could barely see the road, and for one mad moment I thought he was navigating via his satnav, but when I leaned over to look through to the windscreen, I could see that some idiot had already travelled this way, not far ahead of us, leaving the road just about visible. Looking out to the side, I could see nothing other than white, and I began to fear for our safety.

I'd never been to Haxmoor/Noelle/Christmas Manor, whatever the new owner wanted to call it, so I was guessing when I estimated another two miles ahead of us, but with the snow falling faster and faster, I worried that we would not make it, that the bus would run aground and we would be trapped in the vehicle until help arrived. And how long would that take? Airlifting us from the moor was out of the question. Aircraft, even helicopters, needed to be able to see the ground in order to land safely, but according to my best guess, the cloud delivering this deluge was less than fifty feet above our heads. No point asking where I got such an absurd estimate. It was just a number. For all I really knew, the cloud base could have been anywhere between five and five hundred feet above us.

Silence fell over the passengers. They were obviously entertaining the same worries as me. To his credit, Oscar, hunched over the wheel, eyes fixed on the road ahead, chuntering softly to himself, kept the bus moving for what seemed like an age, and then suddenly, he swung the wheel hard left.

At first I thought he was avoiding some kind of obstacle, like another moron who had ignored the weather forecasts, blocking the road, but Oscar kept on driving, plodding along at about five mph, and it dawned on me that he had turned off the main road (although how anyone could describe it as a main road, when it was a) almost invisible and b) not much wider than our street, I don't know) and was on the track leading to Christmas Manor. Either that or he was on another track leading to a derelict farm where we might have to spend the next few days huddled together to avoid freezing to death.

And then suddenly, there were vehicles ahead. Range Rovers, Land Rovers, other 4x4s, and amongst them, a couple of ordinary saloon cars. I suspected that the four-wheel drive vehicles would have struggled to get here, so how on earth did anyone manage it in a Vauxhall Corsa?

Oscar brought the bus to a halt, and was first off. He disappeared into the snowy gloom, and returned a few moments later with other people who were ready to assist us off the bus and into the shelter of the manor.

Ever the gentlemen, Eric and Reggie were first off, and helped us ladies – particularly those wearing sensible flats and thick tights – down.

Having coughed up another small fortune at Sonya's unisex salon, I wasn't about to let the snow get at my hair, so I held up proceedings for a few seconds while I pulled up the hood of my coat and fastened it securely above the chin, under my nose, leaving only my eyes and nostrils at the mercy of the weather.

I stepped off the bus with Reggie's assistance, my boots sank into soft snow, and a young man, whose name I would later learn was Zachary, took my hand and guided me along for about twenty yards before the towering bulk of the house appeared through the snow and the gloom, and the welcoming double doors of the entrance beckoned me in.

Risking a quick glance upwards, I noticed a few Christmas lights making a futile effort to penetrate the grim weather. What a waste of electricity, especially with prices so high.

When we were children, mother would often take my brother and me to see Santa at one of the town centre stores. When the weather was bad like this, stepping out of the snow, slush, rain, bitter cold, and into the sparkling, fairy tale atmosphere of a department store grotto, was a magical transformation and I had the same experience now. One moment, I was shivering inside my topcoat, my eyes and nose, lashed with snow, skin frozen into rigidity, my boots crunching on the ground where it had begun to pack, and the next moment, I was inside a lavish lobby, bedecked with all things Christmas: a giant tree, baubles gleaming in the halogen lighting, fairy lights flickering intermittently, large and ornate decorations dangling from the ceiling, tinsel spread everywhere with complete abandon, a giant Santa chortling, 'ho-ho-

ho' and 'Merry Christmas' in turn, four-foot gnomes, complete with Christmassy attire, giving out yuletide songs, the staff uniforms sprinkled with holly (fake), many of them wearing party hats, neon signs around the walls beaming out messages of goodwill, a giant TV screen showing Christmas scenes one after another, the whole ambience forming a cacophony of festive welcome and joy which would hurl a little girl like Bethany into pleasure overload.

While the menfolk stayed back at the bus, presumably unloading the trailer, I was left with Beryl and Olivia when we were approached and greeted by a tall, handsome man, his formal, reception tailcoat lacking any kind of Christmas adornment.

"Good morning. Allow me to introduce myself. I'm Lyle Noelle, proprietor of Christmas Manor. If you can bear with us for a few minutes, while Mr Reitman gets here, I'll arrange some tea or coffee, and then we'll get you checked in." He gestured towards the range of comfortable seating and tables to one side of the lobby.

I needed it. The coffee I mean, not his unction. Not for the first time in my life, I felt like cursing my husband's perspicacity. Dennis was notorious for not listening to me, and I was equally renowned for disregarding his advice. When he got it wrong because he hadn't listened, he didn't seem to care, and to be honest, when I ignored him and he got it right, it didn't trouble me unduly. For once, however, I wished I'd taken more notice that morning, and said no to Eric… a fortnight ago when he first mooted the idea.

It was too late to worry about it. I was here, and at least we'd arrived in one piece. The journey from Haxford was, to my way of thinking, one of the most dangerous I'd ever endured in my life. I remembered a time in Tenerife when we visited the volcano, and as we were making our way up the mountain by bus, I looked down on a vertiginous drop to one side of us, and said to Dennis, "What happens if the bus rolls off and falls down there?"

He replied with his typical candour. "You stick your head between your knees and kiss your Barcelona goodbye."

That journey was nervy. This was frightening, and right then, I really didn't care how long we had to stay there. I wouldn't go back down that hill until such times as the snow was gone, and if that was sometime in the New Year, then fine. That was how long I would be here.

It was complete nonsense of course. If nothing else, I couldn't afford the prices this place charged, and anyway, Dennis would never allow me to stay that long. He would come and rescue me like a knight in shining armour… or in his case, a man in greasy overalls and driving a clapped-out wrecking truck. He knew, you see, knew that I would never spend Christmas away from my family, and one way or another, he would get me home. Besides, he was an absolute glutton and there were only so many meals Naomi could afford to cook for him.

I spent the next few minutes chatting to Beryl Reitman, cautiously staying away from the subject of the perilous journey, and talking about our various plans for the forthcoming celebrations. She and Eric were going down to London to see relatives for the season, Olivia would be with her boyfriend, the same Tim Farrell who was sat with her on the bus, and I told Beryl of my plans to spend it with the family. We had all but exhausted the topic and the coffee had helped thaw us out, when Eric, Reggie, Tim, and the rest of the gang arrived with our luggage and the plethora of equipment they were going to set up in the ballroom.

My little suitcase was in quite a sorry state, covered in rapidly thawing snow, but I knew that piece of luggage. It was watertight. You could chuck it in the sea and none of the clothing inside would be affected.

After a few words with Lyle Noelle, Eric called us together, and ushered us through to the ballroom, with Lyle following.

Once we were ensconced around a couple of tables, he went into his announcement. "Right, people, I'd like to introduce Lyle Noelle, the owner of Christmas Manor, the man we're pulling out the stops for." He focused on the technicians. "We have our work cut out this afternoon, gentlemen. We need to get all the systems rigged and operational before six this evening. Beryl, Olivia, Christine, Reggie, I'd be glad of your help in testing the sound balances once we have everything set up. Between now and then, you're welcome to catch up on some sleep in your rooms." He turned to Lyle. "Is there anything you want to say?"

"Not really, Eric, other than welcome to

Christmas Manor. If I may just clue you up, aside from the entertainers, many of the guests are important buyers and sellers in the hospitality industry, and we're hoping to impress them to such a degree that they'll be happy to recommend our place to their customers. I really appreciate you pulling out the stops for us. The next few days are important for the Manor, and to put no finer point on it, the staff, all of them local people, depend on our getting a good report from these people for their jobs. I'm relying on you guys and I'm confident that you can do the job for us. Thank you."

It sounded like a bog standard flannel to me, and I noticed that he echoed Eric's 'pulling out the stops' metaphor. Our leader seem to appreciate his words, and with the formal introductions out of the way, we were issued with room keys, and Zachary, my saviour in the snow, showed me to my room on the third floor.

I recall Eric telling me they'd built a large extension onto the rear of the buildings, but I was housed in one of the older units overlooking the front. When Zachary left my case in the room, I offered him a pound, but he refused. "Tipping is not allowed, madam. Well, obviously, we can't stop guests offering, but we're not allowed to accept."

I pressed the coin into his hand. "If you don't tell Mr Christmas, I won't."

At that, he left me to it and I looked around the room. Despite being in the older buildings, it constituted unashamed luxury. No wonder Noelle was charging over three hundred pounds a night. Dennis and I once stayed in a luxury hotel in

Paphos, Cyprus, and that was upmarket, but it was nothing compared to this. A four-poster bed, armchairs which I swear looked more comfortable than the expensive three-piece suite in my front room, a highly polished escritoire under the only window, three radiators which helped maintain a temperature of about twenty degrees, tea and coffee making facilities on the dresser, and several large mirrors where I could check my appearance before stepping out.

The Christmas theme predominant in the lobby and ballroom was present in the room. On one wall was a shiny print of Santa flying through the night on his sleigh, one of the mirrors was surrounded with fairy lights, and the other edged with tinsel, and sprigs of holly (also fake) were dotted here and there. Even the room service menu was littered with Christmas motifs.

The opulence extended to the bathroom, where a large, half sunken tub stood alongside a separate shower cubicle. The washbasin had the requisite shaving mirror, and overhead lights, and all the necessary bits and pieces for some serious pampering were spread about the shelves.

Returning to the room, I opened and unpacked my small case into the drawers and wardrobe, and in the latter, I found a travel iron. I might just need it, too. I would have to make a judgement on that when I assessed the state of my new gown.

I made myself a cup of tea, took a chair by the escritoire and gazed through the window. I don't know why. I couldn't see anything. It was just a sheet of white, and the only things which were clearly visible, were a few snowflakes which settled on the window before melting. As for the rest of the landscape, I couldn't see further than half a yard... but that was a wild guess. Like estimating the cloud base during the latter part of the journey, for all I knew I could be seeing anything from several yards to a few inches.

It was hard to believe that I could be so cold having walked just a few yards from the bus to the hotel lobby, but I was fully thawed when I was shown to my room. A cup of tea and sitting close to the radiator under the window soon completed the job, and with the clock reading a little after ten, praying that the weather wouldn't shut down communications, I took out my phone and rang Dennis.

"Hey up, lass. You made it up there then."

"Of course. I'm ringing you from the hotel, and I suppose you're tucked up in your cosy little office."

"Wrong. I'm in the Snacky having breakfast."

This had the immediate effect of annoying me. Why was he feeding himself in a warm canteen while I was freezing in the snow? Well, I was freezing before I thawed out.

I threw it back at him. "You never warned me how cold it was."

"Yes I did."

"No. You told me there was a blizzard coming. You didn't tell me how cold it would be."

"Well, a woman of your experience, I figured you'd have guessed it for yourself. I meanersay, snow's cold, isn't it, so it stands to reason that you'd be cold walking to and from the bus. Is it as bad as I said up there?"

"Worse. You might have to come and rescue me."

"Well, don't hold your breath. It's getting bad down here, I'm gonna struggle to get home, never mind get up to Haxmoor. Ring me later, let me know how you're getting on."

And with that he rang off, leaving me even more irritated. With my attempt to blame everything on him backfiring, I would have to find another target to vent my irritation.

But that could come later. I gazed across the room at the huge double bed. I was up early that morning. Why shouldn't I?

Five minutes later, I was smuggled beneath the duvet, drifting into welcome sleep.

Chapter Five

I was woken by a phone call from Eric just before one o'clock, telling me that they were heading to the dining room for lunch. "Don't bother to change, Chrissy. We'll be doing some work on the sound systems after we've had a bite."

It was advice I didn't need. I had no intention of changing until the evening anyway. I rolled out of bed, slipped into my jeans, dragged my T-shirt over my head, put on a cardigan, and sliding my feet into a pair of comfortable slip-ons, made my way down to the ground floor.

The dining room was situated on the opposite side of the lobby from the ballroom. It was about the same size – voluminous – but obviously, cluttered with tables and the usual flood of Christmas decorations. Our team had commandeered a table for eight tucked away in one corner, and I tagged on to a queue behind Reggie Monk, shuffling along to help ourselves to cold cuts, salad (in the middle of a blizzard??) boiled and roast potatoes, even chips. With a couple of slices of pressed beef, and a few potatoes, I joined the rest of the crew, and looked around the room in amazement.

It wasn't full, but most of the tables had people

sat at them.

"How did they all get here?" I asked. "It was a struggle for us, and we only came a few miles. How did these people get here? Did they have a large fleet of troikas to ferry them up from town?"

It was Reggie who answered. He aimed his knife at a rotund, middle-aged man a few tables away, a man dressed with simple, expensive scruffiness. "I was talking to George Reynolds an hour ago," Reggie said. "Financier. Worth more than a bob or two. And he was telling me that most of these people shipped in yesterday. One or two on the day before. We were the last to arrive."

"Literally," I said. "Judging by the weather, I can't see anyone else following us, can you?" I munched on a piece of beef, swallowed it, and asked, "So who is this Reynolds? Did he sink money into the place, or something?"

Reggie nodded. "A few hundred thousand, so I'm led to believe. He's quite well known in the big smoke."

"But nobody in Haxford has ever heard of him." The comment came from Beryl Reitman and was laced with a compound of acids.

I decided not to rise to it, and instead aimed for general discussion. "Forgive me for being a bit of a numpty, but I thought the place didn't officially open until Christmas Eve."

"It doesn't," Eric told me. He waved around the room. "Aside from travel expenses, none of these people have paid a single penny for the next three days of their stay. As Lyle explained, they're senior people in the hospitality sector. Directors of travel agencies, senior editors of hospitality themed magazines, travel correspondents from some of the broadsheets. The kind of people Noelle needs to get his message across. He's relying on them for goodwill."

I knew of course. Eric had told me weeks before. Nevertheless, I still gaped. "This shindig must be costing him a fortune, then. Noelle, I mean."

"About sixty grand according to my information," Reggie said. "I suspect that Lyle looks upon it as an investment. Impress this crowd and they can put a lot of visitors his way."

The little cliques around the table dropped into their personal conversations, and I carried on with my meal, lending half an ear to the debate between Reggie and Eric on the merits of location recording, but while they waffled on, I had my eye on the waitress making the rounds of the table, and delivering drinks from a trolley like the ones they use on aeroplanes.

Short, blonde, busty, with an impertinent smile upon her face as she went about her duties, I had the feeling that I knew her, but she was one of those people I couldn't pin down. I'd lived my whole life in Haxford, as a consequence of which I knew many people even if I couldn't always put a name to them, but something told me that I should know who this girl was. I was certain of one thing: she was not a member of my family, close or extended.

The problem nagged at me for many minutes, until she finally arrived at our table offering red and white wine.

While she stood opposite, serving Tim and

Olivia, she looked across, her face broke into a broad smile, her cheeks coloured slightly, and she said, "Hello, Mrs Capper. Nice to see you here. I knew that these people were from Radio Haxford, but I didn't realise you worked with them."

"Yes. I, er…" I pulled myself together. "I'm sorry, but you have me at a disadvantage. I'm sure I should know you, but I can't remember your name."

"Velda. Velda—"

"Grimes," I cut her off. "Velda Grimes. Lester's little girl."

I heard Reggie mutter something like, "Not so little from when I'm looking," but I ignored him.

"I don't see much of my dad," Velda said. "Not since him and Mam split up, but I think he still works with your Dennis, doesn't he?"

"He does, and I see him quite often when I visit their workshop."

Velda busied herself pouring white wine for Tim, red for Olivia, and as she did so, she said, "I heard about what happened to Dennis. Is he all right now?"

"Fit as a fiddle, complaining like nothing ever happened."

She held up the bottle. "Would you like a drop of house plonk?"

I passed. "I don't want to interfere with your work, Velda. We'll see if we can catch up later on, eh?"

We were through lunch by two o'clock, and we repaired to the bar for a quick snifter before moving into the ballroom, where technicians had rigged up the systems.

Tim, our sound genius, was allocated an alcove, where he would be curtained off from the audience, and it was to there that he moved while Reggie took the little stage. Eric stationed himself in one distant corner of the room, positioned his wife in another, and left Olivia in the middle, close to me by the entrance.

Tim faffed about with his various control board, gave Eric a verbal thumbs up over handheld radios, and Reggie, sat at the microphone, went into an ad lib.

"There was a young woman of forty, whose habits were fearfully naughty, and when she was told, she said I'm not old, in a voice that was ever so haughty."

Eric gave Tim the thumbs up, Beryl put her fingers to her ears and shook her head, and from the door Olivia simpered and nodded. There was a brief debate between Beryl and Eric over the handheld radios regarding what she could and couldn't hear, followed by another exchange between Eric and Tim, some more faffing with the control boards and Reggie was ready to go again.

"There was an old geezer from Wapping, and in public his pants they kept dropping. He turned up in court, said the trousers I bought, are too big and they fall when I'm shopping."

I didn't find this verse any funnier than the first, but this time Beryl heard it okay and gave it the thumbs up, although I noticed that she did so with a frown of disapproval which I thought was aimed at Reggie's crude limerick.

Olivia shrugged again and nodded and Eric gave

it the all clear. "All right, Reggie. We're good on your voice. Let's have some music coming through the pipes. Chrissy, love, we'll get to you in a minute or two."

I nodded. I was already bored and I'd only been there five minutes. Now I was bored and terrified.

With his typical lack of refinement Reggie selected Slade's Merry Xmas Everybody and a moment later, I saw Tim wince and rip off his headphones as the noise almost blew out his eardrums. While the music played, Eric walked around the ballroom, pausing here and there to listen. When he got to Beryl, he stopped and there followed a few moments of debate between the two, after which Eric made his way to the podium, looked over Reggie's list of music and chose a different track.

Slade stopped and then came the opening strains of Beethoven's 6th, the Pastoral. I wasn't a particular lover of classical music, but this was one piece I knew, one I'd always found relaxing.

Eric waved at his wife and daughter and indicated that they should wander round the room listening from various areas.

While this was going on a woman ambled into the room. I reckoned her to be about forty years of age, the lean face heavily made up with an excess of shading around the eyes, and her jet black hair cropped and styled, she reminded me of Servalan in Blake's 7, a sci-fi TV series from my youth. She was wrapped in a white fur coat which I hoped was fake, and had the kind of look on her face that suggested the naughty, haughty woman from

Reggie's first limerick.

"How I absolutely loathe Mozart." She delivered this pronouncement in tones of upper class pomposity, the kind of voice which said, 'I am of the utmost importance and you will heed my every word. Failure to do so will incur intolerable pain, poverty, degradation, possibly even death. You have been warned'.

"It's Beethoven," I told her.

"Oh. Ah. Yes. Of course. But I still loathe Mozart. I'm Diana Delancey."

She said it as if I was supposed to register her regal superiority, but for all it meant to me, she might as well have announced herself as the bag lady from Cobble Street.

"And I'm Christine Capper," I replied.

"You're one of the runners for these radio people, are you?"

"No. I'm their star turn. The mystery woman."

She looked so far down her nose that I swear she must have clear view of her chin, and for a moment I was tempted to check the sole of my shoe to make sure I hadn't trod in any reindeer poop.

"So what is it you do?" I asked.

"I am an internationally recognised soprano."

"Oh. Right. The Sopranos. My husband used to watch the series on TV." If she was so capable of looking down her nose, I felt this remark was sufficiently well targeted to come out through her nostrils, and I was right. She wandered off in Eric's direction, and I'm sure I heard her utter the word, 'peasant', for which I vowed I would get her. Well, you would, wouldn't you? Just imagine someone

58

called you a peasant because you'd rather read *Bella* than *The Lady*. You'd be up in arms, wouldn't you? But one could hardly smack her in the mouth in a posh hotel like this.

As she commandeered Eric's attention, it did occur to me she might have said 'pleasant' or even 'resonant', but on reflection, neither word went with the face she gave me, an expression which could be likened to someone sucking on a lemon before downing a cup of stewed tea, laced with washing up liquid.

Our director did not appear any the more pleased than me to be the focus of her attention, but he was far too polite to say anything, and it caused me to wonder about this woman's assumed air of importance. Aside from a brief mention from Eric when we sat at Terry's Tea Bar, I'd never heard of her, but there was nothing particularly fresh about that. I'd never heard of Liz Truss until she became Prime Minister, nor Rishi Sunak, her successor. In fact, thinking about it, I'd never heard of Cameron, Blair, or John Major, until they grabbed the keys to Number Ten.

From the side of the room, I couldn't hear what was being said, but a moment later, Reggie shuffled through the various pieces of music on his machine, and Madame Muck took the stage, the music began to play and she sang the famous Queen of the Night aria from Mozart's Magic Flute.

Not that I knew it was the Queen of the Night aria from the Magic Flute. All I could hear was her ah-ah-ah-ah-aah-ing and oh-oh-oh-oh-ohh-ing in the upper registers, to the point where I felt the glassware in the dining room might crack, by which I mean the glassware still in the dining room forty yards and at least two walls away from the ballroom.

It was Beryl who told me it was from the Magic Flute, and also that it was by Mozart, and yet Little-Miss-I'm-so-Important had just told me she loathed Mozart. In that case, why was she expounding his musical genius at a pitch and volume calculated to shatter the windows and let the blizzard in? Personally, I think she was just showing off, letting me know that she was more important, or possibly noisier than I could ever be.

Whatever the reasons, the screeching, albeit musically accurate to within millihertz of its calculated tone, began to get to me and I was on the verge of walking out, when Eric signalled to Reggie to cut the music.

Diana Delancey was none too happy about this, and she gave Eric a similar look to the one she had given me. I couldn't hear what she said, but it didn't begin with a plosive consonant, so it obviously wasn't 'peasant'. I tried to think of other demeaning names you could call someone, which didn't begin with a B, P or an M. Within seconds, I had a head full of colourful epithets, none of which would be suitable for mixed company.

There was a brief and apparently curt exchange between Tim and Diana before Madam Snob wandered off, swept majestically past me and out of the ballroom, and Eric signalled me to join Reggie on the stage, the boredom evaporated, the terror increased, and my knees turned to jelly.

It was ridiculous, I told myself. Now that Lady Snooty was gone, the only people in the room were those I worked with twice a week – Beryl excepted. I wasn't nervous when they came to my conservatory, I wasn't nervous when I sat in the studio with Reggie, so why should I be nervous? More important, if this was how I felt right now, what would I be like in front of a large audience later in the evening?

Reggie sorted me a chair, in front of which was a music stand, with nothing on it, and the microphone hooked to the top of the frame.

"Right, Chrissy," Eric said. "We've had the Queen of the Night, let's see how we manage with a softer, more seductive voice like yours."

Seductive? Me? I doubted that Dennis had ever described it as such, especially when he was cooking a pan of chips that time, forgot all about them and almost set fire to the kitchen wallpaper. Correction, he did set fire to the kitchen wallpaper. Another ten minutes, and I swear the entire house could have gone up in smoke.

I took the chair and adjusted the microphone, and then stared at the empty music stand. "Eric, I don't have anything to read. My laptop's up in my room."

"Ad lib," he advised me. "It's only a sound test to make sure we have the balances right."

"Yes, but what am I going to say?"

"It doesn't matter. Do you know the soliloquy from Hamlet?"

"You mean, to be or not to be?"

"That's the one. You know it?"

"No."

61

He paused to give the matter a moment's thought. "Tell you what, do you have a script in front of you when you record your vlog every week?"

"Yes."

"Well, what about the opening? I mean, it's the same every week, isn't it?"

"Yes. Roughly the same, apart from the sponsors."

"In that case, run through that. And if you have to go over it a few times, that's all right."

I made a point of adjusting the microphone again, cleared my throat, and began to speak.

"Hello and welcome to Chrastine Kipper's goings and goings... No. That's not right. Sorry, Eric."

He took a deep breath, and for a moment I thought he was going to lose his rag, and bawl me out, but he didn't. "Just relax, Christine. Trust me, you'll be fine."

Just like him, I took a deep and shuddery breath, let it out with a slow count of three, and then began again.

I had to repeat the vlog opening lines several times, before he got the thumbs up from Beryl, Olivia, and Reggie who had taken Eric's place in one corner of the room. And with the time coming up to 3 o'clock, our boss declared himself happy.

"We're all set, people. The time's your own now clear up to 7 o'clock, when we'll see you at dinner. There's dancing from eight until nine, when Diana Delancey takes over. Chrissy, you're front and centre at ten, and Reggie you'll be on cue at eleven

62

to take us into the wee small hours. For now, get yourselves back to your rooms or into the bar if you prefer, but don't get drunk. Thanks, everyone."

Chapter Six

One of Dennis's biggest complaints was the time I took to get ready when we were going anywhere. All I can say is it's a good job he wasn't with me at the Christmas Manor.

Once back in the room, I pinched another hour and a half of sleep, then took a shower, primped my hair, put on a layer of slap and eyeshadow, then climbed into my dress, and stood admiring myself in the mirror for a few minutes.

It was a chiffon, V-neck, A-line, floor length dress in burgundy with translucent, patterned half sleeves, and a built in bra which didn't show any cleavage, and it was enhanced by a pair of matching, block heels, and clutch bag. The entire ensemble cost me just short of two hundred pounds, but I told Dennis it was just over a hundred.

There were two reasons for this little white lie. First, he almost had a fit at a hundred pounds. If I'd told him the truth, he would probably have suffered a coronary. Second, by the time the credit card bill came in, he would have forgotten all about it, or if he did query it I could accuse him of buying a new socket set and ratchet drive. And if he did pose the question as to how come Fab Fashions was selling socket sets and ratchet drives, well, I'd have to deal with that situation as and when it came up, but I could probably persuade him that they were diversifying into hardware and DIY.

Looking in the mirror, I came to the logical conclusion. I looked perfect. Best of all, there was no one else there to argue with me.

I looked even better when I pinned on the various bits and pieces of plastic, glass, and diamante. Peckish, ready for a feed, I had a few words with Dennis on the phone, and at a quarter to seven, I picked up my clutch bag and made my way down to the dining room.

There was no one to welcome or guide me, no maître d'hotel, and I stood in the doorway for a few moments, seeking my Radio Haxford colleagues, when a man I recognised as George Reynolds, sidled up to me. I knew who he was because Reggie and Eric pointed him out earlier, but never having heard of or spoken to him, I didn't realise how crass he could be.

"What's a tidy bit of stuff like you doing in a place like this?"

I gave him a glare as cold as the bitter weather outside. "I haven't been called a bit of stuff for about thirty-five years, Mr Reynolds, and the last person who described me as such, was a self-centred, ignorant idiot who was only interested in getting into my pants... Pretty much like you."

Confident that I had made my point, I looked around the room again, spotted Reggie Monk's head of black hair, and wove my way through the tables to join them.

Eric stood and slid my chair back for me to sit

down. "You're looking the part, Chrissy."

"Yes, well, according to George Reynolds, I'm looking more tart than part."

Reggie cackled. "Sounds about right. He does have a bit of a reputation for fooling around with women."

"Not this woman, Reggie."

The meal of veal cutlets in red wine was perfectly prepared and presented, although a little rich for my usual tastes (and no, my usual taste did not amount to egg and chips). Along with sparkling, light-hearted conversation from the rest of the team, it went down very well, but I was conscious of a rising knot of tension in my tummy. The terrifying thought of appearing and speaking before a live audience was beginning to get to me… again.

Even worse, my memory seemed to be going. "Oh my God, I've left the laptop in my room."

"Not to worry," Eric reassured me, and swung his attention to his daughter. "Olivia, once we're through with dinner, could you nip up to Christine's room and bring her laptop down?"

Olivia agreed, and I had this sudden, horrifying vision of my laptop in bits and pieces all over the floor. I had always been convinced of her gormlessness, but to be fair to the girl, I'd never seen her actually drop any electronic equipment, with the possible exception of her mobile phone. Giving the matter some wider thought, I also realised I had never actually seen her lifting or carrying any electronic equipment, and a vision of my mangled, busted laptop materialised once more in my head.

Dinner was over by quarter to eight, and along with the other guests, we made our way to the ballroom. This time, our table was reserved, tucked tight into the corner, close to the little screened off alcove where Tim would soon be hard at work.

As the crowds began to enter, I handed Olivia my room key, Reggie took the stage, and dimmed the lights, before pulling on light dance music. No Abba, no head-banging, no punk rock, not even a little Beatlemania, but the kind of bland, Victor Sylvester and Mantovani stuff my grandmother used to listen to in the days before television. Not that I was old enough to remember such days, but the tale came from my mother so I assumed it was true.

As if demonstrating his approach to serious matrimony, Eric took his wife to the floor for a waltz, and I had to admire him. It wasn't often that Dennis and I were invited to formal do's like this, and when it came to sweeping me round the floor, Dennis was less skilled than he was sweeping round the carpet with the Dyson, and he wasn't much good at that. The best we could come up with was a smooch, but Eric and Beryl demonstrated perfect footwork, and their presence on the dancefloor encouraged others to join in.

Olivia returned with my laptop, which was (mercifully) in one piece, and as she sat down watching her mum and dad moving gracefully round the floor, I noticed Diana Delancey appear at the entrance, and look around, the familiar look of contemptuous disdain plastered across her face.

As if to prove that he was determined to live up

to the reputation Reggie granted him, George Reynolds intercepted her, an easy smile upon his face. I wouldn't normally have bothered, but after I'd given him short shrift, I was interested to see how Dracula's bit on the side coped with him.

She didn't disappoint. She said something to him, and instead of him walking away as he did when I knocked him back, his face assumed an appearance of something approaching anger. He said something back, she retorted, he said even more, augmenting his words with plenty of finger-pointing, and she made to bite his finger off.

Lyle Noelle appeared and insinuated himself between them, only to receive a mouthful from Diana. Now he took the hump with her, and obviously gave her both barrels. When Reynolds tried to say something, Noelle turned on him too. Watching this from the wrong side of the ballroom, I was tempted to get up, cross over there, and listen in, but even as I thought about it, the group split up. Diana turned on her imperious heels, marched out of the room, Lyle gave Reynolds another salvo, and then followed her, and as if deciding that the argument was not yet over, Reynolds himself went after them.

It was a scene that practically shouted major bust up in the offing, and I was desperate to get out there, lend an ear to the battle, find out what it was all about. And why not? A calling such as mine, whether vlogger, private eye, or wannabe radio presenter, demanded a high level of nosy parkerness. Of course, I didn't move for the simple reason that if they spotted me, and frankly it wasn't so much if as when considering the gown I was wearing, they would drop the argument, and put on the pleasant faces of coming Christmas.

I did notice that all three were gone quite a long time. Victor Sylvester gave way to Strauss, and he stood to one side for (I think) Tchaikovsky, before George Reynolds reappeared, wiping his hands on the seams of his dinner suit. A couple of minutes after that, Lyle Noelle put in an appearance and began to make the rounds of the room, stopping to talk with people here and there, obviously ensuring that everything met with due satisfaction, thereby enhancing his chances of top drawer reports. It was noticeable that he gave our table a miss.

Then, for some reason best known only to technicians and perhaps God, the sound system turned crackly and the lighting began to go haywire. Onstage, Reggie and Eric faffed around with switches and buttons, but when Reggie's declaration of merry Christmas everybody turned into 'Erry…is… ass...ev…ody' Eric began to panic. All the gnomes and Santas and everything were working fine, so it was obviously only our system. And then, when the lights froze, Eric rushed from the floor towards Tim's cubbyhole, threw back the curtain to reveal Tim, knelt behind his bits and pieces, fooling around with… well, I don't know what he was fooling around with, but it was somewhere near floor level rather than higher up. The two men exchanged brief words, Tim's a little sharper than Eric's, and our director came away, and closed the curtains again.

"Doesn't Tim mind being posted to the back like

that, Olivia?" I asked the soundman's girlfriend.

"I think he's used to it, Mrs Copter. From all I can gather, he's never been in front of the microphones in any studio, and he isn't when we come to your place. He was the main man at the recording studios where he worked before. A nunnery or something."

I rather doubted this, but refrained from saying so. A young woman who could change my name from Capper to Copper to Copter was more than capable of changing master disc to monastery to nunnery. Not that I was aware of a recording studio called master disc. I just grabbed the phrase out of thin air… a bit like picking it out of Olivia's brain.

She was still talking. "He's always been in the background and I think he likes it that way."

"And what about you and him?" I asked. "Getting serious, is it?"

She gave out a nervy little laugh. "Not really. I mean, it's a bit early, cos I've only known him a couple of months. We've had a few dates, but I don't think Mam approves. Tim's like fifteen years older than me. I mean, I like him, and he's ever so good to me, and he's incredibly, er… fit if you know what I mean."

Of course I knew what she meant. I just didn't want to hear about it is all. Seriously, how old did this girl think I was? I restricted my answer to a fly comment. "I think I can remember."

"It's the age difference, you see? Mam's already said that when I'm in my forties, Tim'll be pushing sixty. Do you think a big age difference matters, Mrs Clapper?"

70

Before I considered her question, it occurred to me that 'Clapper' was getting awfully close to 'Slapper' and I had to nip this one in the bud. The girl couldn't help being thick, could she, but if she referred to me as 'Slapper' then I'd be strongly tempted to slap her.

"It's Capper," I told her. "But you know, you can call me Christine." I figured that she would be slightly less confused by my given name than she was by my surname. Having cleared up this conclusion, at least to my mind, I focused on her query. "I'm not sure whether a large age difference matters, Olivia. My husband's a year younger than me, so it's not something I've any real experience of, but I think what matters in a relationship is love and trust. Do you love Tim or is it too early to say?"

"Probably." She left it at that, leaving me completely at sea. I didn't know whether she loved him or whether it was too early to say.

The one thing I could say in favour of these distractions was that they took my mind off the prospect of appearing before the audience in a little over an hour's time. With the end of the brief chat between Olivia and myself, that terror began to return, hands shaking, heart fluttering, spirits sinking. I had seventy minutes before I sat on the podium, read from my laptop, and made a complete and utter fool of myself.

I consoled myself with the thought that for now, we had to sit through Diva Delancey and her shrill warbling. Maybe that would be enough to damage the eardrums of the crowd so they might not notice my fumbling, mumbling, staccato performance.

The clock moved inexorably towards the hour, and as Reggie faded out the music, Lyle Noelle took the stage.

"Good evening, ladies and gentlemen, welcome to the Christmas Manor Hotel. I hope you've all enjoyed your day, and you'll enjoy the entertainment we have lined up for you over the next couple of days. Right now, I'd like to get that entertainment under way, so please put your hands together and welcome the lead soprano of Opera Modern, Diana Delancey."

As he applauded he gestured towards the double doors of the ballroom, most people – me included – looked in that direction, expecting them to fly open, and Lord Snooty's female counterpart sweep in.

Nothing happened. Well I say nothing. After a sizeable pause, Noelle repeated his introduction, and began to applaud a second time, but still Diana Delancey failed to put in an appearance.

And then suddenly, she appeared... Only it wasn't her. It was Velda Grimes, and instead of heading towards the stage, she circled the ballroom, and came to me.

She was in a flood of tears, her hands and the front of her white, frilly apron covered in what looked like blood.

"Mrs Capper," she wept, "I need your help."

I was acutely aware of the room's focus on us. Tim Farrell must have been aware of it too, because he tracked the spotlight over to our corner.

I ignored it all and concentrated on Velda. "Whatever it is the matter?"

"It's Mrs DeFancy. She's dead."

Chapter Seven

Velda made no effort to keep her voice down as she announced the terrible news, meaning most of the nearby tables heard, and in a matter of seconds, a rhubarb murmur of excited conversation spread around the room. At the same time, Lyle Noelle hurried across the floor to join us.

"You mean Mrs Delancey," I corrected Velda's error, an inadvertent impression of Olivia. She nodded and I went on. "Try to be calm. Tell me what happened."

"She's in the ladies and she's dead. There's blood everywhere."

Lyle Noelle concentrated on the girl. "What have you done?"

"I haven't done nothing, Mr Noelle. Mrs wossname. She's in the toilet. She's dead."

"And you're covered in her blood. Well, don't think you'll get away with this—"

I cut him off. "Mr Noelle, you cannot accuse this young woman outright. We don't yet know what's happened." I got my feet. "Show me the way, Velda."

"Just who the hell do you think you are?" Noelle demanded. "This is my hotel, and I—"

"I'm Christine Capper, that's who." I left it at

that, hoping that I'd said it with sufficient emphasis to persuade him there was nothing more to be said.

Velda led us from the ballroom, out into the lobby and one corner where the facilities were located. She pushed open the door, I stepped in, inviting her to follow me, but she shook her head. A moment later, I understood why.

Diana Delancey lay on her side, a large gash to the left-hand side of her throat. Her neck, shoulder, the upper half of her gown, and the floor around her was awash with blood. It occurred to me right away the lower half of my very expensive kit would be swimming in blood too if I wasn't careful. I knew what I had to do, but I saw no reason why my Fab Fashions top of the range clobber should end up covered in blood and guts. I couldn't get home to wash and iron it, and even though it was burgundy in colour, the blood stains would still show. I thought about hitching it all the way up and tucking it into the waistband of my tights/knickers, but that, I realised, would crease it so much that they would show. In the end, with a skill to match that of your average contortionist, I pinched my gown at the waist, and lifted the floor-hugging hem to knee height, and gathering the excess up in one hand so that it didn't fall again, I bent over Diana (bent not crouched) and applied a timid thumb and finger to her wrist. I don't know why I bothered at all. It was obvious that she was dead, but I needed to make sure. No pulse. That confirmed it.

I turned to back out of the room, and found Lyle Noelle stood behind me. "Outside, Mr Noelle."

"Now listen—"

For the third time in as many minutes I cut him off. "This woman has been murdered and this is now a crime scene. You need to secure the entrance to make sure no one else comes in until the police forensic team have finished their work."

"The police? Who's to say we need the police."

I let out an exasperated sigh. "I am a former police officer, and I know what I'm talking about. This isn't the first suspicious death I've encountered. She has been murdered."

"You don't know that."

"Oh. You think it's suicide, do you. You think she was so cheesed off at being here that she decided to cut her own throat in the most appalling manner?"

"Well… It could have been an accident."

"While she was shaving? I have to say, she didn't look as if she had that heavy a beard when I spoke to her this afternoon. Get it into your head, Mr Noelle, she was murdered, and we need to get the police out."

He fumed for a moment. "This is not going to do my reputation any favours."

I pointed at the dead woman. "She's not having the best of evenings either." I took out my smartphone. "I'll speak to a couple of my former colleagues at Haxford police station. Now for the last time, we have to get out of here and secure this door."

As we stepped out into the lobby, we found a small reception committee waiting for us, amongst whom were Reynolds, Eric and his wife, Reggie Monk, and Olivia.

75

While I rang Mandy Hiscoe, Noelle rounded on Velda. "I don't know what prompted you to do this, young lady, but you are in serious trouble."

"Stop accusing, Mr Noelle," I warned him.

"Accusing who of what?" Mandy Hiscoe's bright and breezy tones came across the airwaves. "Great to hear from you, Chrissy, but why are you ringing. I thought you were out at some big thrash on Haxmoor. Are you just calling to make me jealous?"

At last I could get a word in. "I am at a big thrash. The Christmas Manor Hotel, and we've had a murder."

"Well, it's different, I'll give you that. Now do us a favour, Chrissy. Stop taking the mick."

"I'm not joking, Mandy. We have a dead woman in the toilets, and you need to get a full team out here."

The urgency in my voice transmitted itself to her, and she was silent for a long moment. "You have two chances, Chrissy. Slim and none. You know how bad the snow is up there?"

"It was rough when we came through it this morning."

"Yes, well, it's never stopped. As far as I'm aware, it's still coming down, and Haxmoor Lane is currently under something like a foot of snow. Maybe not quite that much. The ploughs are out, but they've no chance of getting through at least until tomorrow and I wouldn't lay bets on that if the snow doesn't stop."

If diva Delancey's racket was not music to my ears, this was even worse. "So what are we supposed to do?"

Again I was greeted with silence. After a minute, she came back to me. "Okay. First off have you got a wi-fi and broadband signal up there?"

I put the query to Noelle, and he replied, "We're between Holme Moss and Emley Moor, and we have a mast on our roof. That'll take care of mobile and wi-fi signals, and our broadband is fibre optic and as far as I know it's underground. As long as everything is fine down in Haxford, we'll have a good signal here."

I relayed the information to Mandy, who by this time had made up her mind.

"Okay, Chrissy, here's how it goes. You are our eyes and ears on the ground. You need to set up videoconferencing software through the broadband. You'll need to take plenty of pictures of the crime scene, and if we can't get to you until tomorrow or the day after, chances are, you'll have to make the initial enquiries."

I wasn't having that. "I'm not a copper anymore, Mandy. I don't even push my private eye services these days."

"Did you kill this woman?"

"I was tempted, but no I didn't."

"In that case, you're the only person Paddy Quinn will trust. The minute we're done, I'll speak to Paddy, and chances are he'll ring you and want you online within the hour. Any suspects?"

I glowered at Noelle and then cast a sympathetic gaze upon Velda. "We have a young woman covered in blood, but it's unlikely she carried out the crime. I think she just discovered the body. But I will interview her. Beyond that, no, there's nothing yet to suggest anyone."

"All right. I'll let you get on with it. You know the script. Get plenty of pictures of the crime scene, and the dead woman, and email them to me."

"Which is all very well, what do we do about the body? If it's going to be a day or however long before you can get here, she's gonna be pretty high by the time you arrive."

"Difficult, I admit. Best thing you can do is try to wrap her in something, blankets or even Clingfilm, or whatever, and see if there's a freezer where she can be left. Failing that, does the place have a decent, cool cellar? As a last resort, put her in a room, and leave the room locked up until we can get there. I'm sorry, Chrissy, but you're the man on the ground."

"Or the woman on the ground, as the case may be," I retorted. "All right, Mandy. I'll make whatever arrangements I can, and the moment Mr Noelle can sort me some workspace, I'll set up a Zoom connection."

I cut the call, turned to Lyle Noelle, and related everything Mandy said to me. He took instant umbrage.

"First, I don't know what gives you the right to take charge of anything, second, it's obvious that this girl is the guilty party." He aimed a shaking finger at Velda.

"It wasn't me," she screamed. "I found her like that, and I thought she was drunk and all the red stuff on the floor was wine. When I crossed to her I slipped and fell in the wine, but it wasn't wine. It

78

was blood." Velda began to cry. "And that's how I got covered in it."

"Calm down, Velda," I insisted before rounding on Noelle. "And you, stop accusing. If you want to know what gives me the right to take charge, it's the police, and should you want to argue about it, try taking it up with Detective Inspector Quinn when he gets through to us. But before that happens, let me warn you. Paddy Quinn eats people like you for breakfast. He won't be impressed by your wealth, status, or your arrogance. Like it or not, Mr Noelle, I am a former police officer, and I know what I'm doing." I looked to Olivia. "Could you take Velda off to one side, somewhere quiet, while I get changed and go back in there to take photographs?" I nodded at the toilet door. "After that, Velda, I'm going to need to speak to you." I swung my attention back to Noelle. "And you, Mr Noelle, need to make some kind of arrangement for moving the body and blocking this toilet door. You'll also need to find me somewhere where I can work, and let me establish a video connection with Haxford police." I pointed at the toilet door. "Beryl could I ask you to keep everyone out of there until I get back."

She nodded and asked, "Where are you going?"

I frowned. Hadn't I just told everyone where I was going? I fingered my gown. "I'm not dressed for a murder inquiry."

I didn't wait for any more objections, but hurried up to my room, threw off the Fab Fashions finest, and dragged my jeans and jumper and flats on, then made my way back down to the lobby and pushed my way back into the toilet, where I took out my smartphone, and began to take pictures from several angles. Aware of most of what the forensic people would require, I also crouched down to take several close-up images of the wound to Diana's neck.

Once I was satisfied, once I had about two dozen images, I came out of the toilet, to find the crowd dispersed, and two porters, one of whom was Zachary, holding a couple of blankets, obviously ready to make their way into the toilet, wrap the woman up and carry her out. Neither man looked particularly enthusiastic about the task, and Noelle, having backed off a little, was still clearly disgruntled.

"Absolutely no way am I putting a dead body in any of our freezers, and she's not going in the cellar. I have some expensive vintages stored down there. We'll take her back to her room, and lock the door."

"Fine. When you've done that, will you make sure that the key comes to me, please."

His temper was beginning to get the better of him. "You're doing it again. What—"

"As of this moment, Mr Noelle, I am responsible for what happens with regard to the inquiry into this woman's murder. I need to ensure that no one, absolutely no one at all, gains access to that room and her body. Vital evidence, you see, and we must make every effort to ensure it's not disturbed any more than we need to in order to move her. As and when the police finally get here, they will take charge of it. Until then, I'm in charge, and as I said, if you're not happy about that, take it up with DI

Quinn when we get to speak to him. But think on. I'm saying 'please'. He won't." I gestured at the toilet door. "You're free to go in and bring the poor woman out, and after that the door needs to be locked or otherwise immobilised. I'll be with Velda Grimes."

As I walked away, leaving Noelle and his people to their distasteful task, I was intercepted by Eric and Beryl. "Chrissy, what's going on? Beryl's told me about Diana, but you're supposed to be on stage very soon."

"It won't happen, Eric. The police can't get here, and they've asked me to take charge of the crime scene and initial inquiries until they can." I gave him a nervous chuckle. "You wanted me to talk about a mystery, and here we are wrapped up in a real live one. If you'll take my advice, get ready to make some kind of general, calming announcement, and keep the music going, maybe switch to karaoke or something. I can tell you this. No one will be allowed to leave this hotel until the police get here and they've spoken to them."

Eric gestured towards the exit. "Looking at the state of the snow out there, no one could leave anyway. Is there no chance they could get a helicopter in?"

"I don't know. I'll speak to Paddy Quinn about it, but from what Mandy Hiscoe told me, the snow is still coming down, and don't helicopter pilots need to see the ground before they can safely land?"

He ground his teeth. "I don't know, but from all you're saying, we're trapped?"

"Yes. And whether you like it or not, whether I

81

like it or not, I've been lumbered with this. Now if you'll excuse me, I'll have to speak to Velda." I focussed on Beryl. "Any idea where Olivia took her?"

She gestured towards the dining room. "It was the quietest place. The only people in there are the staff tidying up after dinner."

We found them literally just inside the dining room, sat to one side. Velda was clearly very distressed, and Olivia seemed to me not to be too sure of what was going on but she had managed to secure a glass of water for the girl.

"How is she?" I asked.

"Bad," Olivia replied. "She keeps saying she didn't do it."

"And I would agree. The amount of blood in the toilet, Velda would have been showered in it if she'd killed the woman." I concentrated on the poor girl. "Now, Velda, no one is accusing you of anything, but the police have asked me to carry out the initial enquiries. Can you tell me exactly what happened?"

"When she was due on stage, Mr Noelle spoke to the people on reception, asking where she was. Someone had seen her go into the toilet, so they asked me to go in and remind her that she was due in the ballroom. When I went in, I saw her on the floor, and I thought she was just drunk, only I wasn't sure, so I went to check on her and that's when I fell. I didn't do it, Mrs Capper. I was only gonna wake her up. I shouldn't have. I should have come out and told Mr Noelle, I should have—"

"All right, all right. Try to keep calm. There was

no one else in there when you went in?"

"No. Well, I don't know. One of the cubicles was shut, and there might have been someone in there, but I didn't look. I was panicking."

"That's okay. We all understand. Did you see anyone hanging around in the toilet before you went in?"

"No."

"And no one came out as you were going in?"

"I didn't see no one."

I patted her hand. "Not much more I can ask right now, but depending on what the police instruct me to do, I might have to speak to you again, Velda. For now, you can go."

We watched her leave and Beryl expressed her opinion. "That girl is innocent."

"I think so, too, but I think proving it, or worse, proving who's really guilty will be a devil of a job."

We rose to leave the dining room, and it suddenly occurred to me just how unprepared I was for this kind of eventuality. I had my laptop, and I could establish communication with Paddy Quinn, but I was here for a couple of nights of relaxation and entertainment, even if I was delivering part of that entertainment, and I had no notebook with me other than a small diary, and that would hardly be adequate for what I knew that Quinn would ask of me.

While I was ruminating on the matter wondering whether I could scrounge a loose leaf, A4 notepad from reception, my smartphone rang.

"Christine Capper."

"Christine, it's Paddy. Mandy rang me ten

83

minutes ago. Before we get into what you've done and what you can do, let me bring you up to speed on the weather situation. We have absolutely no chance of getting to you tonight, but the snow is forecast to stop by midnight, so we should be with you tomorrow."

"Slightly more positive than what Mandy said, Paddy. Someone did ask me if there's any chance of getting a helicopter here to airlift people help?"

"No chance. According to those in the know, the cloud base is somewhere just over a thousand feet. You're about eleven or twelve hundred feet. In other words, you're right in the middle of the cloud, and God knows what the cloud ceiling is, but we're talking thousands of feet. Even if the snow stops, until the cloud clears, we can't get anyone to you by air. We're monitoring the weather, and we've already got snowploughs working at the lower levels. The moment the blizzard passes over, we'll be concentrating on clearing a route up to the hotel so we can get you all away. For now, you're the only person I trust who can carry out some initial observations."

"I get that, Paddy, but I'm already meeting resistance, particularly from Lyle Noelle, the man who owns the place."

"Don't worry about him. I'll speak to him in a few minutes. Did you get the necessary photographs?"

"Yes. The moment we're through talking, I'll hook my laptop into the hotel's wi-fi, and get them off to… Who will I send them to? You or Mandy?"

"Send them to Mandy's email address at

Haxford station. Now listen to me, Christine, and this is important. Don't get overambitious. In other words, don't put your neck on the block. If you have any thoughts, any observations, fine, we'll listen to them, but initially, it's more important if you can get us some idea of the woman's history, who she was and wasn't involved with. You got that?"

I heard what he was saying, and I knew I would go further than he wanted, but it wasn't worth the argument, so I agreed. "Yes."

"Good. You're there with the Radio Haxford team, aren't you?"

"Yes."

"Right, I'll speak to Eric Reitman. I wanna see if we can hook something up so that I can speak to the staff and guests, ensure that they know I've put you in control. That'll probably take a little while to set up, but in the meantime, you should do what you can to help people keep calm."

"And who's going to help me keep calm, Paddy?"

He laughed. "I have every confidence in you, Chrissy. I know we don't always see eye to eye, especially when you poke your nose in where it doesn't concern you, but for once, you're poking your nose in with my official approval."

Chapter Eight

Paddy terminated the call, and I stared at my smartphone, my mind filling with a sense of dread and disbelief.

I served as a police officer for eight years, but I never aspired to CID. I was an old fashioned community constable, a beat bobby, and even though I had assisted with enquiries into serious incidents, even one murder as I recalled, it was purely from a uniformed point of view. Fingertip searches, keeping the general public back from crime scenes, making tea for distressed victims and their families. It was only many years after leaving the police that I went for my private investigator's licence, and since then I'd garnered some investigative skills, but to lead an inquiry like this? Never in my wildest nightmares.

Right away, I determined that I would do exactly as Paddy asked, even though I knew I wouldn't. I would go too far. I would make an effort to 'crack the case' before the police could get to Christmas Manor.

I left the dining room filled with this sense of panic which put my fears of speaking to an audience into some kind of perspective. I had been nervous about that. I was terrified about this.

I would need some support, and Lyle Noelle was out of the question. He'd already decided that Velda Grimes was guilty, and anyway, I didn't like the man. I could say the same about George Reynolds. He might have influence, he might be of assistance, but I'd seen him arguing with Diana before she was due on stage, so I scratched him and added him to my 'suspects' list. Eventually I settled on Eric Reitman for support.

In his role as program director at Radio Haxford he was calm personified, and even Reggie Monk at his most outrageous couldn't ruffle Eric's feathers. If I needed someone to back me up, he was the man.

When I got back to the ballroom, where Reggie was squawking Irving Berlin's 'White Christmas' into the microphone, I spotted Eric sat in our corner, his phone held to one ear, his finger in the other to drown out the racket coming from Reggie. I couldn't question my colleague's skills as a DJ, but as a singer he would make a perfect sergeant major, ideal for bawling out orders on the parade ground.

Few people were taking any notice of Reggie's appalling voice, although there were one or two couples shuffling around the dancefloor. Keeping to the walls, I made my way round the room and bore down on Eric. As I got near, it became obvious that he was speaking to Paddy Quinn.

"Yes, Inspector. I understand... Yes. Christine's just arrived." Eric gave me an encouraging half smile. "I'll get that arranged, and call the police station at Haxford the moment were ready for you." He cut the call, and smiled again. "Inspector Patrick Quinn, asking me to set up the large screen on stage, so he can address the audience."

"Thank God for that. Eric, I'm going to need someone to help me, someone with sense, and you're the only person I can think of." I waved around the room. "These people will make mincemeat of me... let's put it another way, they'll try making mincemeat of me and I'll end up in more arguments than is good for me... or them. I need someone with some sensible authority to help me out."

"You can count on me, and don't overlook Beryl. I know she may be a bit more reserved than I am, but she's an experienced schoolteacher, deputy head at a large comprehensive. Handling an audience like this won't be much different to handling a class of rebellious teenagers."

I felt a wave of relief wash through me. "Thanks, Eric. You're a star."

I took my seat at the Radio Haxford table, and I saw both Lyle Noelle and George Reynolds bearing down upon us. Neither man looked particularly pleased, and I wondered what business it was of Reynolds. Then I remembered what Eric and Reggie had told me about him. He had a lot of money invested in this place.

And it was Reynolds who went on the attack. "Who the hell do you think you are, woman?"

I prided myself on my ability to keep my temper. I also prided myself on the ability to throw such arrogance back at men like him. "Oh, I'm a woman now, am I? Earlier, I was a bit of stuff."

"Now listen—"

"No, Mr Reynolds, you listen. My boss, Eric

Reitman, is in the process of setting up communications with the Haxford police, and very shortly, you'll be listening to Detective Inspector Patrick Quinn. Any problems you have with my authority, you can put to him. For now, go away."

"I have a sizeable investment in this place."

"And I have a husband and family less than ten miles away, and I can't get to see them. I also have a dead woman, and the police have asked me to assume responsibility for ensuring that the crime scene is not contaminated, and that the people in this room don't club together to dream up unbreakable alibis. For the second time, go away."

Noelle countered this time. "Just what we need. Here we are trying to launch an upmarket business, and we're confronted with a flaming Miss Marple. You have no right—"

It wasn't me who cut him off, but Beryl Reitman. "And you have no right to ignore the murder of a young woman on your premises, Mr Noelle. Nor do you have any right to challenge Mrs Capper, who, with the best will in the world, has been asked to handle this matter by the police."

Noelle was physically shaking and shared his glowering eyes between Beryl and me. "For your information, the Chief Constable is a personal friend, and I'll make sure he knows about this."

"Do give him my regards, Mr Noelle," I said. "And while you're chatting with him, do ask him to pass on my Christmas wishes to my very good friend, Lieutenant Colonel Sam Kalinsky of the Cabinet Office Investigative Services. I'm sure the colonel will be only too happy to advise the chief constable on the legal position regarding this evening's incident."

It was an empty threat. Even if they or the chief constable could get in touch with Sam Kalinsky, his work was so classified that he would deny ever having met me. In fact, considering the high level of secrecy that department operated under, there were no guarantees that the chief constable knew Sam Kalinsky or even the Cabinet Office Investigative Services existed. However, neither Noelle nor Reynolds knew that, and my announcement was sufficient to make both of them back off. Or at least, that's what I thought. In fact, it was Eric's reappearance from Tim Farrell's cubbyhole, that made them move away, and only then because Eric indicated the corner of the stage where he would like a word with them.

As they moved to join our director, I touched Beryl on the arm. "Thank you for that."

"It's no problem, Christine. I'm sure Eric's told you I'm deputy head in a comprehensive, and I teach sixth formers. I'm perfectly used to dealing with arrogant little snots like them."

Although I couldn't hear, I watched the exchange between Eric, Noelle, and Reynolds. There was an awful lot of gesticulation, face-pulling, from the owners of the hotel, and single-minded determination intermingled with semi-apologetic shrugs from Eric, who stressed his words with the occasional, random finger pointing around the room.

I may have come out of the confrontation ahead on points, but that did nothing to minimise my concern over the number of such head-to-heads still to come. Most of the audience, according to Noelle, were important people within the hospitality industry, and I doubted that they would take kindly to a middle-aged, Yorkshire lass challenging them.

On the other hand, Beryl's confidence in her self-reliance bolstered my waning courage. It was tempting to think that I could do with Dennis alongside me, but that was not so. Dennis's idea of diplomacy was a lump hammer. He was about as tactful as an out-of-control thirty-tonne truck. Reinforced by Eric's opinion of his wife, I felt sure that Beryl would be a formidable ally when faced with some of these people.

Reggie finished screeching into the microphone, and looked as if he was about to call for volunteers, when Eric caught his attention and drew a finger across his throat, indicating that Reggie should shut up.

Our director stepped onto the stage, took the microphone, and ran into his announcement.

"Ladies and gentlemen, forgive the interruption to your evening's entertainment, however, there has been a serious incident here in the hotel. I'm now going to ask our technician to bring the screen to life, and let you to listen to Detective Inspector Patrick Quinn of West Yorkshire CID."

From the outset, I was impressed by Eric's calm control. He had made efforts to encourage me in the face of speaking to a live audience, but I figured it was all talk. I realised I was wrong. Here was a man usually hiding and working in the background, but equally quite at home when addressing a large group of people.

He stepped out of the way, the giant screen lit up, there was Paddy, staring into the lens of his webcam, face deadly serious. I put my smartphone into flight mode as he began speaking.

"Good evening, ladies and gentlemen. My name is Patrick Quinn, and I'm the senior CID officer in the Haxford area. I'm sure you're all aware by now that there has been an incident at your location. A woman has been murdered. At the same time, the appalling weather prevents me and my team of detectives from getting to you. I've therefore had to take an unusual step. Could I ask Mrs Christine Capper to take the stage, please?"

I felt my heart leapt into my mouth, and my knees turned to jelly as I left my seat and climbed onto the podium to stand alongside Eric.

Paddy went on, still talking to the audience. "Mrs Capper is a former police officer. She and I worked together many years ago, and I'm well aware of her capabilities. She also a licensed private investigator and is well aware of the stringent requirements surrounding this kind of crime. Until such times as we can get officers to you, I've asked Mrs Capper to take control of proceedings, to ensure that the body has been moved to a secure location, ensure that access to the crime scene is prevented, to make sure that no one leaves the hotel. That latter point may sound slightly ridiculous considering the weather conditions, but I don't want anyone trying to leave on foot. Aside from risking your very life, until you have given a statement to the police, it would be an offence. We cannot say with any certainty when we will be able to get to the manor. It will certainly not be any sooner than tomorrow morning, and depending on the weather, it could be the day after. You have my personal assurance that we're working flat out to get there. For the time being, I must ask you to please cooperate with Christine Capper. Thank you for your attention, ladies and gentlemen. I have a view of you on my screen, so does anyone have any questions?"

Someone from the far side of the ballroom got to his feet and asked a long, rambling question of Paddy which I couldn't hear. I saw my old colleague's features darken slightly. He drew in a breath, paused a moment, and then responded.

"I'm certain that Mrs Capper will inconvenience you as little as possible, Mr Nooney, and no, she does not have the power of arrest, but if I receive reports from her of any kind of non-cooperation, you may rest assured that I will ask the questions when I get there, and you will answer me or face the consequences. Have I made myself clear on that matter?"

Mr Nooney, whoever he was, sat down, and by the look on his chubby face, he wasn't entirely happy with the implicit threat in Paddy's reply.

As if reading my mind, the inspector went on. "Just to reiterate the situation, ladies and gentlemen, we are not conscripting Christine Capper or anyone else into the police service. She is not a police officer, but I know her well, and she has a wealth of experience in this kind of area. All I'm asking of you is please cooperate with her. Anyone who does not, will face a lengthy and uncomfortable interview when me and my team of detectives get to you."

Paddy paused once again in order to see if there were any more questions. When none came forward, he concluded his announcement.

"Thank you for your attention, ladies and gentlemen. Initially, I would like anyone who knew the victim, Ms Diana Delancey, to come forward and speak to Mrs Capper. The more information we can gather about the victim, the more likely we are to arrive at a satisfactory conclusion." Paddy glanced down at what I assume what a notebook from which he was taking prompts. He looked back into the camera. "I have one last point to make. It's entirely possible that this attack was random and unprovoked and that there is an individual amongst you who is seriously disturbed and as such, highly dangerous. Please take care. If you must leave the crowded areas, don't go anywhere alone. Ensure that someone is with you at all times. Thank you, ladies and gentlemen, for your attention and your cooperation."

Chapter Nine

Thank you, Paddy. That was the first thought running through my head as the screen went blank. Here we were trapped in a remote mansion, three days to Christmas, and the inspector had just reminded us that we might have a maniac on the loose.

Eric, completely in control of himself, picked up the microphone and began speaking. "There you have it, ladies and gentlemen. In a moment, I'm going to ask Radio Haxford's DJ, Reggie Monk, to carry on playing music, please feel free to take the floor. Could I ask Mr Noelle and Mr Reynolds to find somewhere where they, Mrs Capper, and I can meet in order to organise the way forward?"

We left the stage to Reggie. Eric took my arm, and led me towards the exit, where Noelle and Reynolds were headed. As we made our way round the walls, Beryl Reitman joined us.

"I thought you might need some serious support," she explained, and frankly, I was relieved to have her along. Not that I was particularly intimidated by the two men we were meeting, but I had the feeling that Beryl could handle them at least as well as I could.

Once out of the ballroom, Noelle led us behind

reception, and in through a door marked General Manager.

A spacious, windowless office with several chairs dotted around the place, the centrepiece was what appeared to be an antique, mahogany desk. If it wasn't antique, it certainly should have been judging from the number of knocks and chips in its surface. As always, it generated the urgent need in me to nip home, pick up my dusters and a can of Mr Sheen and give it a good going over.

Noelle waved us into seats, positioned himself behind the desk, and picked up the telephone. After barking a few orders into it, he replaced the receiver, and faced us. "I've ordered coffee. While we're waiting, Mr Reitman, can you tell us what on earth you want with George and me?"

"Simple enough, Lyle. We're trapped. Inspector Quinn made that plain enough. We have sixty guests, one dead body, and a flood of suspicion amongst those guests. We have to do something to keep their minds occupied over the next twenty-four, forty-eight hours." Eric looked to me for support.

"Mr Reitman is correct. Forgive me, but your reaction earlier on, Mr Reitman, and yours, Mr Reynolds, are symptomatic of stress already setting in. And it's contagious. It will transmit itself to your guests, they will get stressed, the number of arguments will steadily increase, and if there's one more incident, it's possible that we could be faced with panic. Over and above any enquiries or observations I have to make, we need to keep these people calm."

"And the best way to do that," Beryl said, "is to keep their minds occupied, entertained."

There was a knock on the door, and at Noelle's instruction, a waiter entered with the tray of coffee, placed it on the desk, and upon Noelle's second instruction, a blunt, "get out", he left.

It wasn't really any of my business, but indulging my legendary inability to keep my mouth shut, I asked, "Do you always treat your staff so rudely, Mr Noelle?" I helped myself to a cup of coffee.

"How I treat my staff is no concern of yours, Mrs Capper. Can we concentrate on what the police have asked you to do?"

I was about to say, 'if you treated me like that I'd leave you singing soprano'. Perhaps not the wisest of observations considering the only genuine soprano in the hotel was lying dead in a room somewhere above us. Before I could utter a word, Beryl got in before me.

"I have to agree with Christine. You really are a most unpleasant man, Mr Noelle, but I also agree that we have more important considerations than your behaviour towards your employees. Eric?"

Her husband had obviously taken the brief, irrelevant interlude to marshal his thoughts. "To get back to what we were discussing," he said as he picked up a cup of coffee, "I think we should continue with the programme of entertainment you had planned, Lyle. Christine was due to deliver her Mystery Hour after Diana's appearance this evening. We can reschedule that for later… if her initial inquiries are complete."

In amongst the furore, I'd all but forgotten about it, but Eric's final words brought back the sheer dread having to deal with it.

Our director went on. "I know you have a masked ball arranged for tomorrow night. What else did you have planned?"

Noelle lounged in his seat, sipping on a cup of coffee. "There's a couple scheduled to entertain us tomorrow afternoon and again in the evening. Carpenters stuff from the 1970s. Harry and Yolande, I think they're called. Keith Nooney is the man to ask about that. Him or his wife, Joan. They arranged the entertainment."

"Couldn't you put them on tonight?" I asked. Anything to get out of talking to the audience.

Noelle's lip curled. "You and your people are taking up the stage. They're not set up, so the answer is, no, we can't."

Something Olivia had said came back to me through my immediate disappointment. Nooney? Nunnery? "Do Mr and Mrs Nooney run some kind of theatrical agency?"

"Not so much an agency, more a booking service. Keith was something in the music industry. He owns a recording studio or something like that, and he has contacts with a lot of entertainers. He was the one who persuaded Diana to perform here tonight. Despite what you or anyone else may think of her, Mrs Capper, she was internationally recognised, and she was an excellent soprano. We were lucky to get her."

"Not so lucky for her," I said. "I'll need a word with Mr Nooney." I bequeathed them an obsequious smile. "Do go on with what you were saying."

In fact it was Reynolds who went on. "Aside from that, you're supposed to be front and centre tonight and tomorrow with your stories." He looked down his nose as he said it and I had to wonder what it was about such people that they could do that so frequently and with such ease. "Hopefully, by then, your local yokels should have the roads cleared and we should be able to get the hell out of here."

Not for the first time, his attitude irritated me. "May I ask, Mr Reynolds, where do you come from? London?"

"Surrey."

"In that case, you won't be familiar with winters oop here in the frozen north. You know. Anywhere north of Watford. They get so bad, we can hardly find the wherewithal to exercise our whippets."

"I don't think I like your attitude."

"And I don't think I like you, full stop. You're trapped, Mr Reynolds. Deal with it."

Eric stepped in to avoid another flame. "Calm down, Christine. You too, George. Between us, we are responsible for these people, and by that I mean responsible for their safety and mental health, not just keeping them warm and feeding them. It won't do us any favours falling out amongst ourselves. To go back to where we started, I would suggest that the best course of action is to maintain the programme of entertainment as it was originally planned, with suitable adjustments to cater for Christine's responsibilities. Food stocks are adequate, are they, Lyle?"

"More than adequate. We bought in for the whole of the Christmas and New Year period. Fresh bread might be an issue, but those were the only food deliveries we were planning on receiving this side of the New Year."

"And there's plenty of booze," Reynolds said.

"Fuel and energy supplies?" I asked.

"They shouldn't be a problem," Noelle said. "Right now, the National Grid is still holding up, but if it fails we have our own emergency generators. And the oil reservoirs for the heating, were full as at yesterday. We were expecting a top up on Christmas Eve and again the day after Boxing Day." He shrugged. "Whether those deliveries will be able to go ahead, we really don't know, but surely the blizzard will have gone, and the roads should be clear by then."

It was a point I had not considered. I didn't want to be trapped here anymore than they did. I wanted to be with my family.

That notion brought a welter of self-pity upon me. Here I was stuck out on the moors wrapped up in murder, dealing with two of the most unpleasant men I had ever encountered, and I was less than ten miles from home. Yet I couldn't get to that home. Visions of Dennis, Simon, Naomi, little Bethany, flooded my mind and I felt as if I was about to burst into tears.

I forced rigid control upon myself. "In that case, I don't know that we have any more to discuss, but I do need a favour, Mr Noelle. I didn't come prepared to get into an investigation, and when he gets here, Paddy Quinn will expect a detailed report. Could I scrounge a notepad from you?"

His reply was as sneering as his general attitude. "I think we can afford that."

A few minutes later, armed with a spring bound notepad, I returned briefly to the ballroom, to collect my laptop, and then made my way to my room. "I have to speak to my husband," I explained to Eric, Beryl, and Olivia as I left.

As I travelled up to the third floor, I sent Dennis a text telling him to get onto the computer and open the Zoom software. I got to the room and plugged the laptop into the mains adaptor. It had been left in hibernation for a couple of hours, and the battery status was already down to 88%. The last thing I needed was for it to die even though that probably would not happen for another twenty-four hours or more. I called up Zoom, double clicked my home link, and a few seconds later, Dennis's face appeared.

It was only then that it occurred to me that I had dialled home and not Simon and Naomi's place.

"Dennis. What are you doing there?"

"You told me to get ready for your call."

"Yes, but I dialled home by mistake. You should be at Simon's."

"You're joking, aren't you? Have you seen the snow?"

I tutted. "When I look out the window, I can't see anything, but the whisper is the snow is about a foot deep up here."

"Well, it's not much better down here. I had a heck of a job getting home, and no way was I gonna fight my way to Simon's, and then fight again to get home. As it is, I had to come home in the wrecker."

The wrecker was an old truck designed for towing anything up to medium-sized vans from breakdown or accident sites. It was basically a twenty-year-old, untidy piece of junk but vital to Haxford Fixers' operation... according to Dennis. The thought of it parked on the drive outside our tiny little bungalow, on a street of equally tiny bungalows, occupied by friendly neighbours, some of whom, could be quite snobbish, sent me into a downward spiral of depression.

Dennis was still talking. "I had to drop Geronimo off. Good Boy could manage – so he said – and Grimy reckons he'll doss in the public bar of the Sump Hole for the night."

Geronimo was Tony Wharrier, Dennis' senior partner, Grimy was Lester Grimes, the third partner and Haxford Fixers' electrical wizard. Good Boy was Greg Vetch, the stand in for Dennis when he was laid up after May's assault. Since then, he'd been made a junior partner.

Dennis was still talking. "According to the forecast, the snow stops in sometime around one or two in the morning."

"Paddy said midnight."

"Paddy got it wrong, then, didn't he? The gritters are out round town, but they can't get up the hills until the ploughs can get there to shift some of the heavier snow."

I frowned. "I thought the gritters had ploughs fitted on the front."

"Yeah, they do, but they can't cope with this depth. Round town, fine, but not trying to climb the hills."

"How did you manage to get up Moor Road?"

"Diff lock." He could see my puzzlement and smiled in that supercilious manner he used when he knew something that I didn't. "Differential lock. Works like a four-wheel-drive, gives you maximum traction and torque on your drive axle. Any road up, you better be prepared for spending tomorrow night up there."

"Which was what we had planned in the first place, Dennis. And it could be longer. Things have taken a turn for the worst."

"Why? What's happened? Have they run out of beer?"

"Don't be daft. Since when would a moorland place like this run out of drink?" I let my irritation calmed. "No. It's much worse than that. A woman's been murdered."

For all Dennis cared I might as well have said some woman had lost one of her earrings. "Just goes to show you, dunnit. You set off for a bit of a Christmas shindig, you end up in a right mess."

"It's worse than you think. Paddy Quinn has appointed me the SIO on account of him not being able to get here."

My husband tutted. "Well, that's what you get. I tried to tell you this morning, and—"

"Are you actually listening to me, Dennis? A woman has been murdered. We can't get the police here, and they expect me to investigate."

"Yeah, well, you were good at it, but you said you were giving it up."

It was worse than talking to Cappy the Cat. He

wouldn't take any notice of me either, but he would pay attention on the offchance of me feeding him. I shifted the subject sideways. "If the snow does stop tonight, what are the chances of the ploughs getting through and police getting here tomorrow?"

"Somewhere between slim and fair. If it stops and doesn't start again, they'll be out early doors, and trying to shift the snow, but it could take them most of the night and the filth should get to you tomorrow morning. They'll need specialist vehicles to handle the packed snow and any ice that might have formed under it, particularly for the journey back down the hill. And before you ask, there's nothing I can do to get you out of there. I meanersay, I'm a mechanic, an auto engineer, not the SAS."

"Thank you, Dennis. As always, you're a model husband. Pretty much like the mannequins they have in the bridal shop window."

"Well, thanks for nothing. At least you've had a meal. I've had nothing yet."

"As luck would have it, there are plenty of TV dinners in the freezer, and hey, don't touch the Christmas cake. It's for the weekend."

Chapter Ten

Dennis cut the connection faster than I could.

Bristling at his offhand manner – in truth, he was always the same when talking about anything other than cars and their engines – I shut the laptop lid, unplugged the adaptor, gathered the borrowed notebook and a few pens, and making sure I had everything else I might need, I left the room, locked the door, and made my way back down to the ballroom, where Reggie was encouraging people onto the dancefloor with some seventies disco music.

There weren't many takers. Reggie himself was jiggling around the floor with Olivia, and I felt sorry for the girl, but on reflection, if anyone had to tolerate his body odour, well, rather her than me.

Most people in the room were ignoring the music, and talking amongst themselves, and it didn't take a genius to work out the main topic of conversation. And just to give you a clue, it wasn't Christmas.

I joined Eric and Beryl, and right away our director's wife, volunteered. "When you speak to these people, Christine, do you need a secretary to take notes?"

"Well, I can do it myself, but might be useful if I

have some support. Would you mind?"

"Of course not."

"Good. I think we need to start with Mr and Mrs Nooney. After all, they booked Diana, so in theory they should know more about her than anyone else."

Eric got to his feet. "Where will you speak to them? Here?"

I stood up, too, and Beryl followed suit. "I think the dining room, the same as we used when speaking to Velda Grimes. It's far too noisy here, and I doubt that Lyle Noelle would allow us to use his office. Besides, for all I know, he might have the room bugged."

Eric nodded. "You to make your way there and I'll bring them through to you."

"Is Eric always this helpful?" I asked as we made our way through the lobby.

"You should know him almost as well as I do, Christine," Beryl replied. "He's forceful when he needs to be, and that's especially when he's talking to the head of station, but most of the time, he jollies people along. As he tells it, you were quite reticent when you first began to broadcast."

"Perfectly true. I was like a kitten having… er, kittens."

We laughed together.

"He does get the best out of people, and I've always insisted that the BBC's loss was Radio Haxford's gain. People listen to him. Think about Mr Monk. Reggie can be quite… what's the word…?"

"Free and easy, out of left field?"

"That's accurate, but I was thinking more in terms of coarse. Look at those absurd limericks earlier when they were testing the sound balances. If it weren't for Eric and other people, Reggie would be like that on air. Were you a listener before you joined them?"

"So-so," I admitted. "My researches and my investigative work used to take me out of the house a lot, so it's not like I was glued to the radio all morning, but I always had Radio Haxford on in the car, and my husband and his partners are regular listeners."

"Dennis, isn't it? The genius of the spanners according to Eric."

I laughed again. "It was probably Dennis who told Eric that."

Stepping into the dining room, we chose the same table we had used earlier, just inside and to the right of the door, and I handed the notebook and pens to Beryl.

"You're worried about this, aren't you?" she asked as she penned in the date. "The police asking you to lead until they get here."

"Is it that obvious?" I sucked in my breath. "Frankly, yes. All right, I'm a private investigator, and I was a police officer, but that was years ago. I've shoved my nose into one or two serious crimes, but I was never CID. I can ask questions the police may not be allowed to under PACE restrictions, but I don't know how much of what I may learn would count in a court of law, and obviously, the people we speak to don't have to answer me."

"In that case, Christine, we must just do our best

and leave the rest to Inspector Quinn when he turns up."

Almost on cue, Eric entered accompanied by Keith and Joan Nooney, neither of whom looked particularly happy to be there.

My initial assessment put them in their early fifties, a similar age to me. The resemblance ended there. I was dressed in a couple of hundred pounds worth of High Street finery, but I guessed his dinner suit cost almost as much as my car, and I don't know where she bought her gown, but it generated visions of one of those hoity-toity shops which put everything on hold and tapped it's corporate feet while waiting for the design of the new king's royal cypher before altering the in-store décor. One of those places where the security wouldn't let a commoner like me through the door.

Both were well built, by which I mean fat. His middle put a severe strain on the cummerbund, but judging from the sweat pouring out of his balding prow and salt and pepper back and sides, he would probably lose a few pounds before the night was over. Her weight problem was less pronounced, and was focussed on her enormous bosom and a brace of shoulders like a front row forward. I assumed the remainder was kept in place by an armour plated corset, and despite their apparent wealth, I felt quite comfortable with my size fourteen (all right, so just lately I was closer to a sixteen) frame.

I was less content with their imperious, irritable attitude.

"Why have we been dragged out of the ballroom?" he demanded and his wife nodded in agreement. "My God, woman, do you seriously think we had anything to do with this?"

"No. I—"

Mrs Nooney cut me off. "The very idea is not only unthinkable but downright insulting, and I shall expect an apology from you and the police."

"No one is accusing you of anything, Mrs Moody… Mooney… Nooney." I was relieved to get the words out even if I did get their surname wrong twice. Served them right. Coming in here with that kind of attitude.

"Then why—"

Beryl came to my rescue with a timely interruption. "I think if you shut up long enough to let Mrs Capper explain, you may find out why we asked you here first."

If looks could kill, Beryl would be impaled and probably pinned to the wall. "I've never been spoken to like that."

I was on the tip of my tongue to say, 'Then you should get out a bit more,' but I controlled the impulse. "We asked to speak to you because we've been informed that you knew Diana better than anyone in the hotel, and we're seeking background information on her."

Keith Nooney ran a chubby hand across one of this several chins as if checking for stubble. "I wouldn't say that. Yes we recorded her a few times, but it's not like we knew her that well."

"And yet you booked her for this do."

"No," he disagreed. "We spoke to her agent and he booked her."

"Oh. And is he here?"

109

"He's spending Christmas at his holiday home," Joan replied. "Barbados." She delivered the last word with an air of snobbish satisfaction which did nothing to endear her to me. Not that she appeared troubled by that, but I targeted my next comment to get up her fat nose.

"Barbados not Bridlington," I said to Beryl, then faced the couple again and gave them a sweet smile. "You've worked with Diana. What type of person was she?"

"Snobby," Keith declared and it occurred to me that with a wife like Joan, he would be an expert on snobby. "Don't get me wrong, she could sing. Voice like a nightingale, and she could hit every note perfectly, but she believed that gave her the right to lord it over everyone."

A bit like your wife, I thought, and again I had to stop myself from saying it.

Keith was not yet through. "Best person to ask is that sound man of yours. Young Farrell."

His announcement took both Beryl and me by surprise. "Tim?" Beryl asked.

"He used to work for us," Keith explained. "Good man, knows his stuff when it comes to acoustics, sound, and music. I was sorry to see him go."

Again, I recalled Olivia mentioning how Tim had worked for a 'nunnery'. "He left or you gave him the order of the boot?"

"A bit more complicated than that," Keith admitted. "Times were hard. He wanted more money but we couldn't afford it."

Rebellious thoughts struck me again. *Forking*

110

out for sequined gowns for your missus, I'm not surprised. "So you fired him? Or he left of his own accord?"

"Ah, well, you see, it doesn't work like that. Guys like him are self-employed, but he'd worked for us consistently for a good few years. We were paying him slightly less than the going rate, and we ran into some cashflow problems. We didn't even have the money to pay him what we owed him, he got another offer and that was it. He went."

I turned to Beryl. "Was that offer from Radio Haxford?"

Beryl shrugged and it occurred to me that she wouldn't know one way or the other.

Joan Nooney opened her mouth to answer, but her husband beat her to it and made my question redundant. "Never in a thousand years. He got a direct offer from some singer. He wouldn't say who, but we figured it was Diana. How he came to be working for a tuppenny, ha'penny set up like yours, I don't know, but I know he had a bit of a thing with Diana for the four weeks she was using our studio."

As he delivered this, I remembered I'd seen Tim talking to Diana after our sound test during the afternoon and the exchange did not look too pleasant. Mind you, would Diana Delancey have understood the word pleasant? Peasant, yes, but pleasant?

That woke Beryl up. "A bit of a thing? You mean he was sleeping with her?"

I guessed that her concern was for her daughter, but Keith, who probably knew nothing about the

111

relationship between Olivia and Tim, laughed. "Sleeping was the last thing they were doing."

He received a disapproving glare from his wife, and Beryl made a lengthy note of the response plus (I think) one or two reminders for herself for when she confronted Tim.

"And this went on for how long?" I asked.

"We don't know," Joan declared. She obviously felt she had left the talking to her husband for too long. "It's not in our nature to enquire after the unseemly habits of our staff."

"Of course not," I commented. "As long as they're not doing it on your front rug."

"Well, really. As if—"

"Please accept my apologies, Mrs Nooney. I was thinking out loud." I gave her another sweet smile. "Is there anything else you can tell us about Diana that might help the police? Her relationships with Lyle Noelle and George Reynolds, for instance."

"You'd have to ask those two about that," Keith said. "It's not my place to say anything."

I took this as an admission. "Oh. So there is something? Only, I saw all three of them arguing by the ballroom exit not long before Ms Delancey's body was discovered."

"Like I say, it's not my place to comment. Ask them."

"Right. I can't think of anything else, but do bear in mind that Inspector Quinn, or one of his officers, will need to speak to you when they get here. Thank you for your help."

Beryl and I watched them leave, chattering between themselves… well, she was talking, he was listening, and although we couldn't hear what she was saying, it was obviously about us and from the look on Beryl's face, I'd say she, like me, did not believe Joan Nooney's opinions complimented us upon our professionalism.

"Not that helpful," Beryl said as the couple disappeared through the door. "Who's next?"

"I need to speak to both Noelle and Reynolds, but I'd like a word with Tim Farrell first."

"You're not the only one, Christine." The stern set of Beryl's features told me I'd got it right when I guessed she was concerned for her daughter, but I still sought confirmation.

"Olivia?"

"Yes. Let's be honest, you've worked at the studio for the last, what, six months?"

"Slightly longer."

"Then you must have realised the Olivia isn't the brightest child in the class, but trust me when I say she's not stupid."

She does more than a passable impression. The thought leapt into my hyperactive brain. "But?" I asked.

"She's naïve and a little slow on the uptake. She sees the world in black and white with no shades in between, and she doesn't always listen. I've heard her call you Capper, Copper and Copter. For long enough she called Reggie Monk, Bunk and even Dunk, which she thought was short for Duncan. Tim wouldn't be the first man to take advantage of that. I don't like the thought of him using her." Beryl's eyes narrowed. "You know what I mean by using her?"

113

"Helping him get a leg up at the studio?"

"No. She couldn't do that because Eric wouldn't let her. I mean using her to relieve his... er... *tensions*."

"Ah. Point taken." I picked up my phone. "Let's see if Eric can spare him."

As it turned out, it was a no go. "I need him in the booth," Eric told me. "The technology is playing up. Could you defer until later tonight or first thing tomorrow?"

"If I have to, but Paddy Quinn will be nagging for updates first thing in the morning and he won't be interested in techno-gremlins. For now, could you ask George Reynolds or Lyle Noelle to join us please?"

Chapter Eleven

Reynolds was the first to join us, and he was not a happy bunny. I go further. He looked ready to tear both Beryl and me apart, and his anger was so obvious that it prompted Eric to stay with us, even though I assured him we didn't need his assistance.

"I've never forgotten any of my police training in self-defence, Eric," I said, "and I'm perfectly capable of dealing with Mr Reynolds should he decide to turn violent."

It was no more nor less than the truth. It was also sheer bravado. I had learned enough to let me handle violent men, but it was thirty years in the past, and George Reynolds was a good ten years younger than me, and to look at him, he was quite fit. Not beefcake, not Mr muscle, but trim, as if he kept himself in peak condition with regular gym sessions.

Even so, I was confident that I could deal with him, especially with Beryl by my side, but Eric elected not to move. I guessed he was more concerned for his wife than me.

Or maybe he was more concerned with what his wife might do to Reynolds if he started acting up. For sure, Reynolds didn't take kindly to any of the exchange.

"I don't consider myself a violent man, but I object to being treated like a common criminal."

"No one's doing anything of the kind, Mr Reynolds," I said, "but the police have asked me to make initial enquiries, and let me remind you that if you don't answer my questions, you will answer them when Paddy Quinn puts them to you. He won't be half as gentle as me." I put on a sardonic smile. "Besides, who would treat you as a *common* criminal? You're a wealthy man. If anything, you'll be an *upmarket* criminal."

It wasn't the wisest thing I could have said, but ever since he referred to me as a 'bit of stuff' I'd been determined to puncture his ego.

His features darkened. "What the hell do you want? Come on. Let's get this farce over."

I maintained my composure. At least, I hope I did. "About ten, fifteen, twenty minutes before Diana's body was discovered, you and she were arguing by the ballroom exit."

"I deny that. I don't think I spoke to her all evening."

"You're lying, Mr Reynolds. I saw the exchange. When you pointed at her, she made as if to bite your finger off. What were you arguing about?"

"You're mistaken. I told you, I haven't spoken to her all evening."

I leaned across to Beryl and in a voice deliberately loud enough for Reynolds to hear, said, "Make a note, Beryl. The suspect persists in lying, despite having been witnessed arguing with the deceased." I faced Reynolds again, and put on my sweetest smile this time. "That should be enough for Paddy Quinn to put the cuffs on you and cart you off to Haxford cop shop, where you can make friends with all the drunks and druggies… the common criminals."

He half rose as if ready to leap over the table and beat me to a pulp, but Eric stepped forward, gripped him by the shoulder, and made him sit down.

"I insist—"

I cut him off. "I'm not interested in your lies, Mr Reynolds. I saw you. You and Lyle Noelle, arguing with Diana at the door before she stormed out. Lyle followed her, and a moment later, you followed them. Now what was the argument about?"

"None of your damned business."

"That may be so, but Paddy Quinn will want to know, and if you refuse to answer him, he really will put you at the top of the list of suspects for her murder. If you want me to help clear your name, Mr Reynolds, keep you out of Inspector Quinn's spotlight, tell me what the argument was about."

"It was personal. Right? Nothing to do with anyone but me and the bag."

I couldn't ignore his abusive reference to the dead woman, but Beryl could and she got her comment in first.

"She was murdered, Mr Reynolds. I guess that's pretty personal."

I seized the point. "That's right. Whether you know it or not, most murders are committed by people known to the victim, and for this to be personal, you must have known Diana prior to this evening. Now, for the last time, tell me what you were arguing about, or I'll mark you down as

117

obstructive and highlight your name for Inspector Quinn's particular attention."

He did not answer immediately. Instead he sat, staring at his hands, fulminating, his lips moving soundlessly, probably cursing me. Eventually, he turned, leaned on the table and jabbed a finger into the top. "I knew her all right. I knew her years ago, before the rest of the world heard of her. She was a chorus singer. I heard her singing, and I knew I could do her some good. All right, so I'm a financier, I put money into business ventures, but I have an awful lot of contacts in a lot of industries, including the theatre. I put her name forward to some friends of mine, and the next I heard, she was starring as Abigaille in Nabucco."

I hadn't a clue what he was talking about, but Beryl understood. "An opera by Giuseppe Verdi," she explained to me.

It still didn't mean much to me, but at least I'd heard of Verdi. I focused on Reynolds. "And this just happened overnight, did it?"

"Of course not." His level of incredulity was spelt out by his sneering tone. "I'm talking of a three or four year learning curve."

"Very good. And what does that have to do with your argument earlier this evening?"

"I reminded her of it. That's all."

"And you tried to extract a price?"

His anger built again. "Nothing of the kind. What do you take me for?"

"After referring to me as a 'bit of stuff' earlier in the night, you really don't want to know what I think of you, Mr Reynolds. However, I'm not

118

concerned with your crass approach, and the police won't be either. All I'm asking is did you try the same trick with Diana Delancey?"

"No, I did not. I suggested a drink after her performance, and she told me where I could shove it."

Considering my brief encounter with the woman, I could see this happening. George Reynolds might be wealthy in the extreme, but if she didn't consider him 'classy', she would have told him where to get off in no uncertain terms.

I focused on the job at hand. "So you've never had any kind of relationship with her?"

"No. And I defy you to prove otherwise."

I gave him yet another friendly smile and spoke in a voice tinged with acid. "It's not up to me to prove anything, Mr Reynolds. I'm simply reporting to the police. They're the ones who will ask the really serious questions. For now, I have only one more question for you. Immediately after your, er, exchange with Diana, she and Lyle Noelle left, and a moment later, you followed them. Where did you go?"

"None of you bloody business."

I sighed. "Again, you're right, but the police will want to know, and if it can be demonstrated that you followed her to the ladies' rest room, you're going to be in some trouble."

He glowered. "I did not go to the ladies. I went to the gents. The lavatory, the smallest room, the khasi, call it what you will."

Beryl made note, and I concluded the session. "Thank you, Mr Reynolds. I'll pass your comments on to Inspector Quinn when he gets here, but do bear in mind, I'm not a police officer, and he may very well want to speak to you in person."

"And he'll get nothing more out of me than you have."

With that, he kicked back his chair, stormed to his feet and tromped out of the room, brushing past Eric so closely than I expected our director's hair to be ruffled in the slipstream.

With a nervy half smile, Eric joined us at the table. "He wasn't very forthcoming, was he?"

"He is seriously in the frame," I said. "It doesn't matter how much he tries to flimflam his way out of it, I saw the argument, and it was a good deal more serious than a woman refusing to accept a drink from him. But it's not our problem. It's one for Paddy and his team when they get here."

"All right. Who's next?"

"Lyle Noelle." I felt my features darken. "I don't imagine he'll be any easier than Reynolds. Tell me, Eric, how well do you know Lyle?"

"Not as well as you may think. I remember him from his younger years when he was working in the City. I was working for the Beeb at the time, and we did a number of interviews with him. That was during the financial crisis of 2008. He'd be in his mid-thirties at the time, one of the coming men in the financial sector. He knew how to make a lot of money very quickly, and there was always some suspicion of insider dealing, but nothing was ever proved. Of course, his father was still alive at the time, Lord Noelle of Haxmoor, and as a sitting member in the Lords, he had quite a bit of influence."

"Did Lyle not inherit the title when his father passed away?" I asked.

"Yes. But he doesn't use it, and as far as I know, he's never attended the House of Lords. He's a businessman, Chrissy. The kind of man who would rather be doing it that talking about it."

Eric laughed at the inevitable innuendo in his final words. Beryl, did not find them funny. "Reminiscent of Tim Farrell," she said.

Eric frowned. "Again?"

Beryl shook her head. "I'll tell you later."

To stop the discussion from side-tracking, I asked, "Can you get Lyle in here, Eric? I don't think he'll be much different to Reynolds, but we do have to speak to him."

"Yes. Of course. Give me a minute. But once you've dealt with him, Chrissy, it's time for you to take the stage, and deliver your mystery hour."

My heart leapt. "I – I thought we were deferring that."

"The slot's been arranged, and the station are going bananas, trying to fill the gap with music while they wait for you to start. I'm sorry. I realise the pressure this business has put you under, but it will have to be this evening."

He disappeared through the doors, and a new, more horrible realisation struck me. Everyone in the ballroom knew who I was and the unwanted duties I was charged with. How much would that knowledge blow my credibility? Everyone in the room would see me as a 'copper's nark' by the time I was through detailing the Graveyard Poisoner, they would be convinced I was really an undercover plod.

That wouldn't apply to my regular listeners in Haxford. They knew me. Thanks to my vlog and my other spots on Radio Haxford, I'd been around for a long time, but the people in this audience were not Haxforders. Most of them probably didn't know Haxford existed until they arrived here the previous day. I anticipated a hostile reaction when I took the stage, and it was exactly what I didn't need considering my ingrained nervousness at the prospect.

I didn't have much time to think about it before Eric returned with Lyle Noelle in tow. Our host sat opposite us in the same seat that Reynolds had occupied, and I could be forgiven for thinking he was George Reynolds in another body. He had the same air of anger bubbling just beneath the surface, the same challenging body language, and a similar scowl sitting to his normally placid features.

I went through the same opening as I had with Reynolds, spelling out the argument between the three which I had witnessed.

"I don't see where our disagreements have anything to do with you, Mrs Capper."

"You're probably right, but I don't think Paddy Quinn will take the same line. After the argument, you and Diana left the ballroom. George Reynolds wasn't far behind you. So I have two questions, Mr Noelle. First, what was the argument about?"

"George and Diana were spitting feathers at each other. I told them to shut up. I was thinking of my guests. They both took umbrage, and tried to bite

122

back. I laid the law down. End of story."

"Fair enough. What were they arguing about?"

"I really don't know. You'd have to ask George."

"We did, and we're not happy with his answers." I carried on before he could come back at me. "Let me rephrase that. I'm not happy with his answers, but I don't count. I'm not the police. I'm simply here to take a few notes and pass them on to Inspector Quinn."

"In that case, Inspector Quinn will have to take it up with George, won't he? I don't know what they were arguing about. I just know I wouldn't tolerate it. George wasn't exactly a guest. He has a sizeable amount of money invested in this place, which means he should have an interest in seeing it succeed. Diana wasn't a guest either. She was here to entertain our audience. If they had some argument between themselves, then it needed to be dealt with in private, not in the ballroom."

Beryl struggled to keep up with the speed at which Noelle delivered his account. I gave her a few moments to catch up, and when she gave me the nod, I tackled him again.

"You left the ballroom at the same time as Diana. Where did you go from there?"

"My office. Where do you think?"

I shrugged. "You own the place, Mr Noelle. As far as I'm concerned, you could have gone anywhere... including the ladies toilets."

"Well, I didn't. You're right, I own the place, and I have to run the place. I went back to my office. Is that it? Can I get back to my guests now?"

"Just one more question."

"I thought you said you had only a couple of questions."

"Another has just occurred to me." I paused. "Can anyone vouch for your whereabouts after you left the ballroom?"

"I don't know. The receptionist, perhaps, but I really can't say. You're just going to have to take my word for it."

"And I will, but I can't guarantee that Paddy Quinn will be that charitable." I could think of nothing else I need it to ask him. "I'll make sure I pass your account on to Mr Quinn when he gets here, but as I said, I'm not the police. Quinn will probably speak to you again."

He got to his feet and concentrated on Eric. "May I remind you that Mrs Capper is due on stage with her Mystery Hour... when she's done playing policewoman."

Eric bequeathed him an obsequious smile. "It's all in hand, Lyle. All in hand."

Chapter Twelve

If I was trembling when Paddy Quinn called me to join Eric on stage an hour or more previously, it was nothing compared to the way I felt when I set the laptop up on the lectern and took a seat strategically located so that I could read the laptop screen but it did not block the audience's view of me.

The moment Eric made it clear what was happening, I had to fly back up to my room, run Lyle Noelle's travel iron over my slightly crumpled gown (I know the iron wasn't his personal possession, but considering his attitude as 'lord of the manor' it's apposite) and change into it. By the time I got back to the ballroom, not only were we behind schedule, but I was out of breath.

There was some fussing and faffing while Eric and Reggie set up the microphone close enough for me to be heard, close enough for it to pick up and broadcast via Radio Haxford, but not so close that plosive consonants like 'B' or 'P' would sound like a mini explosion.

(If you're paying attention, you should be aware that this is the second time I've mentioned plosive consonants. I'm sorry, but it's necessary. They might help my rubbish lip-reading skills but in

terms of talking through a mic, they can be problematic... as can my next observation.)

Over the years of recording with my webcam and the months of working with the radio techs, I had learned to breathe quietly. Sucking in a rush of air would cross the ether and listeners would imagine someone doing something unmentionable to me. So would the audience, especially after seeing me rush into the place all hot and bothered. When I sat down, I was trembling so badly, my breath coming in short, sharp, barely-controlled gasps that unless I established some control fairly quickly, those same listeners might well imagine they had tuned into an obscene phone call. I had visions of them faffing with the radio to find the correct station..

The microphone was still switched off when Reggie said, "Just relax, Chrissy. You'll be fine."

He was leaning close to me, adjusting the microphone when he said it, and I copped the full blast of his body odour and halitosis, both of which encouraged 'run for it' rather than 'take it easy'.

Eric stood in front of me, and began to count down from five. When he got to three, he shut up and finished the count with his fingers.

And then came the music. *In The Hall Of The Mountain King* from Grieg's *Peer Gynt*. You know the piece I mean. The one that goes. Du-du-du-du du-du-du, du-du-du, du-du-du, du-du-du-du-du-du-du, da-da-da-dee-dee. Spooky, yes, and in my opinion, more suited to creepy tales from the crypt than criminal investigations.

And then the voice of Stella Briggs, night anchor

on Radio Haxford during the week, talked over the music. "Ladies and gentlemen, make yourselves comfortable and prepare to listen to true tales of serious criminal events in…. Christine Capper's Mystery Hour."

The music reach a crescendo, then stopped so suddenly that I wondered (prayed) that the sound system had gone. No such luck. Eric cued me and a tiny red light on the microphone stem told me we were live.

In radio, even a couple of seconds of silence is like an eternity. I think I got to about five seconds before Eric prompted me with a whispered, "Christine, you're on. Talk to them."

"Good evening, gentlies and ladies men. I'm Christine Capper, and tonight I'm going to tell you all about the Gravepoison Yarder…. I beg your pardon, the Graveyard Poisoner."

That was it. I was lost. Jill Bleaker's script was there before me on the laptop, but I couldn't see it. The words were just a blur. I don't know how many of the audience were laughing, I don't know how many were staring in astonishment. All I could see was the Christmas tree, the fairy lights dotted around the room, tinsel dangling from the walls and ceiling, and through the open doors of the ballroom, the life-size Santa ho-ho-ho-ing… probably having a good old chuckle at the gormless opening I had just delivered.

Frozen almost into immobility, I salvaged what little of my brain was still working and asked myself, what would I do if we were recording this in my conservatory at home. Go again. That's what.

But I couldn't do that here... or could I?

I recalled the first time I'd given evidence in court. A judge, a jury, barristers, clerks, all focused on me in the witness box. Was this more intimidating?

Well, yes, it was, quite honestly, but I got through that, and struggled through cross examination from the defence brief. If I could cope then, I could do it now.

I ignored the laptop, stared out across the sea of faces, and smiled. "Forgive me. I'm not really used to sitting and talking before a live audience. So let me start again. I'm Christine Capper, and as tonight's sad events have revealed, I used to be a police officer and then I became a private investigator. I'm well known in the Haxford area for my investigative work and for my weekly vlog. But I'm going to talk to you about real crimes which I investigated, and I'm going to start with a series of events which culminated at Christmas time last year, when I was involved in a police investigation, and instrumental in solving the case of the Graveyard Poisoner."

From there, everything just flowed. I used Jill's script as a guide while I ran through my memories of the case, and the way I'd been dragged into it after being asked to investigate the theft of expensive library books, which coincided with an attack on Benny Barnes in his bargain basement. A serial killer, the Graveyard Poisoner had been active for over two years when we eventually closed the case down and I'd always been rightly proud of my involvement.

Which was more than could be said of Paddy Quinn. If he told me once, he must have told me half a dozen times to keep my nose out, but I ignored him. Contrast that with the way he had asked me to take the lead in this evening's killing of Diana Delancey.

Before I got too far into the tale, I had the audience ooh-ing and aah-ing at the revelations, chuckling along when I threw in my little jokes, and by the time thirty minutes had passed, I felt as if I'd been doing it all my life, and it was at that point that I silently congratulated Eric and his team... not forgetting Reggie, and believe it or not, Olivia. Not that she did anything mega, but she now and again, when a small round of applause was called for, she walked along the front of the audience carrying a placard which I later learned, read, 'APPLORZ'. That caused me to wonder whether part of the audience's laughter was at the expense of my jokes or her spelling.

When he first mentioned the idea to me, Eric insisted that they were looking for forty three minutes. All right, he actually said three-quarters of an hour, but the script was timed at forty-three minutes which allowed for one minute of intro and another minute of exit credits. Trouble was this was billed as an hour on Radio Haxford, and allowed for something like twelve minutes of adverts and a short news bulletin. How was that supposed to work?

I was well into the tale of the Graveyard Poisoner and that allowed my mind to freewheel a little, which in turn helped me realise how they were working it. It was billed as 'live' on the radio, but it wouldn't be. It would be live-ish. The entire thing was being recorded – Tim Farrell's responsibility, no doubt – and the studio would have a tiny hold on it; say one minute. That would give them scope to cut the 'live' broadcast at any time, go to the commercials, and then pick up again after.

It was hardly rocket science, but it had never been explained to me and yet I had worked it out, and having done so, I felt, for the first time since I met with Eric on the sixth, that radio was my future. Radio Haxford at least. Nothing too grand, although, as he said at the time, there was no telling where it might lead.

That thought came as I was heading into the denouement of the Graveyard Poisoner story, and with it came another spurious thought. I wasn't sure how long Reggie Monk had worked for the station, but it hadn't led to greatness for him. Maybe, I thought, he had no ambitions in that direction. Maybe he was content as the morning anchor on Radio Haxford. Maybe he was worried this ex-wives – both of them – might show up demanding money with menaces if he became a household name beyond the Haxford town boundary. Or most likely, for all his years at the station, no one had heard of him, and the few that had would rather they hadn't.

As I reached the conclusion, the microphone became crackly. I broke the golden rule of radio and tapped the head a couple of times. Aside from bringing a glower from Eric, it produced no change.

Our director rushed to Tim's cubbyhole in the

130

corner, and finding no one there, start to faff with the equipment. I knew Tim was AWOL because I'd seen him sneak off a few minutes previously. As Eric tried to put matters right, our sound man made his way back and it appeared to me as if he was skulking along the wall side. His hair looked wet. Not that he had much hair, but the bit that he had was damp... or maybe it was just his pate shining through, reflecting the strong lighting. He also looked as if he was limping, or maybe that was just because he really was slinking in an effort to keep a low profile.

While I carried on reading out the ending of my tale, I could overhear their debate.

"I needed a leak, man," Tim protested, only he didn't use the word 'leak'. "And it's the weather causing the gear to act up."

"Get it put right," Eric insisted in a fit of temper I'd never seen nor heard from him in the past.

I don't know what he did, but Tim corrected the problem in no short order, and Eric stepped up onto the platform. "I'm sorry to interrupt, ladies and gentlemen, but for the benefit of our radio listeners, I'll have to ask Christine to re-read the last two or three minutes of the story."

He gave me an encouraging smile and I backtracked to a point I'd reached before the mic went wrong, and re-read it.

Less than five minutes later, I shut down the laptop screen, faced the audience and declared, "And that, ladies and gentlemen, is the story of the Graveyard Poisoner."

I received a round of generous applause and it

131

was spontaneous. No one needed Olivia's badly spelled placard, and some of the crowd stood to applaud me. It gave me a warmth of feeling as I basked in their appreciation, a glow of satisfaction I hadn't experienced since the last time Dennis and I … yes, well, never mind.

I came off the stage to a reprise of *In The Hall Of The Mountain King*, and Reggie took my place. "A fantastic lady, let's hear it again for the fabulous Christine Capper." I had to return to the stage and take another bow, before Reggie got the late show under way with *Jingle Bell Rock,* and whether it was my talk which had relaxed them, I don't know, but in seconds the dance floor began to fill up.

With Reggie leading the night, I joined my colleagues at the corner table where Beryl gave me a private round of applause. "You were brilliant, Christine."

"I told you," Eric echoed. "You're a natural, Chrissy. Now come on. What are you having to drink?"

Usually, when I was out, I would be driving, and I wouldn't drink. No driving to or from Christmas Manor, so… "Gin and it, I think," I said, taking my seat next to Beryl. "But I feel like a fraud, Eric. I mean, I haven't actually been asked to do anything else… have I?"

"Lost Friends, but that's tomorrow afternoon, and it's only about half an hour."

"And you're forgetting that the police have left you to lead their murder investigation," Beryl said.

"I just checked outside," Olivia chimed in, "and the snow's easing a bit, so maybe Mr Skin and his team will make it tomorrow."

"Quinn," I corrected her.

Her brow knitted. "Oh. Mr Skin and his Quinn?"

While Eric toddled off to the bar, I decided I was having too good a time to bother with the debate.

Olivia, however, had other things on her excuse for a mind. "Tim's in trouble with Dad. He went for a wee and the microphones went wrong. I don't mean they went wrong cos he wee'd on them, but he wasn't there to mend them for you, Crispin."

What was it I said earlier about how she would find it difficult to get my given name wrong?

"When you've got to go, you've got to go." Turning to Beryl, I went on, "And I need a word with our Mr Farrell."

I was convinced that she was going to say something like, 'You're not the only one' but before she could, Olivia piped up again.

"He did put them right, Justine. He says it's the weather making them break down and with the snow stopping, they should be all right from now on."

I smiled at the girl in that sympathetic manner you reserve for your average simpleton. "I know, Olivia, but that's not what I want to talk to him about."

"Oh. What then?"

I exchanged a furtive glance with her mother, and then patted Olivia's hand. "It's nothing you need to worry about, love."

Chapter Thirteen

As it happened, getting a few minutes with Tim wasn't a problem because Reggie was working the turntable and the sound man wasn't really needed. Reggie could adjust the volume from his stage array and if the speakers began to give out, Eric had enough know-how (gleaned from his years at the Beeb with some help from Tim) to correct the matter, at least until Tim could get back.

Beryl and I took him off to the dining room where we could talk in comparative quiet. We made ourselves comfortable, Beryl ready to take notes, and judging from the look of thunder on her face, take him apart once we were through quizzing him.

"So what is it you want?" he asked. "It wasn't nothing to do with me, the way the mic broke down. I told Eric. It's the weather and there ain't nothing I can do about that."

For the first time, I realised that he spoke with a strong London accent, which made sense if he had worked for the Nooneys.

"It's nothing to do with the mics," I told hm. "It's to do with Diana Delancey."

His face underwent a rapid change from umbrage to defensive. I could see it in his eyes, especially the way they darted back and forth between Beryl and me.

"I don't know nothing about her death."

"But you did know her," I challenged him.

"In the biblical sense," Beryl added in a voice laced with nitric acid.

"That's not true."

I took up the attack. "It is according to Keith Nooney. You were the recording engineer during her studio sessions, and during the four weeks that she was there, you were closely involved with her on a personal level. And earlier today, I saw you exchanging words with her after she'd finished screeching into the microphones."

He stared glumly into a glass of water.

"Tim," I urged, "we're not accusing you of anything. We're trying to get some background on Diana. All we're asking is that you tell us what you know."

Now he played with the glass, turning it round and round on the table, as if he expected a different view from the opposite sides. Eventually he looked up, took a slug from the glass and nodded. "All right, yes, I knew her and yes, I was sleeping with her for a while."

"According to Nooney the last thing you were doing was sleeping."

The comment came from Beryl and Tim bit back at her. "You know what I mean." He focussed on me. "She made all the running, not me. You don't know her. She was snooty, high class tart… well, she thought she was high class. In fact, she came from this end of the country. Heckerwide or somewhere."

135

"Heckmondwike," Beryl translated, even though I didn't need it. "Between Dewsbury, Bradford, and Huddersfield, not far from where we live."

I didn't need her to tell me where Heckmondwike was either, but before I could comment, Tim was talking again.

"She was common as muck," Tim went on, "but she could sing, and by sing, I don't mean warbling the latest Taylor Swift on karaoke. She had a superb voice. And she was quick on the uptake. I mean, those opera composers worked in Italian, German, even French and Spanish, and Diana didn't speak more than a few words of those languages, but put the lyric in front of her and she'd have it off by heart in twenty-four hours. And she had stage presence. That... that Reynolds geezer spotted her and gave her a leg up, and she was worth it. But she never forgot how to get what she wanted by using other, natural assets, and I reckon she paid George Reynolds back in kind, if you follow my meaning." He paused to fume for a moment. "And, yeah, she took me to her bed and we had a good thing going for the four weeks she was working in the Nooneys' studio, but the minute the job was done, she called it a draw. Cleared off to Milan or somewhere and I never saw her again until we got here today." His face descended into a dark scowl. "And when I spoke to her, she didn't want to know me. Told me to... well, I don't use language like that in front of women, but let's just say she had no problem dropping back into her working class roots."

There was something not quite right about what he said, something that did not gel, but before I could put my finger on it, Beryl piped up.

"So you latched onto my daughter." Her annoyance was growing with every word.

"Olivia is over twenty-one and knows what she's doing, Mrs Reitman. I'm not gonna say we're serious, but we have feelings for each other."

"With you doing most of the feeling I should imagine."

"Now, listen—"

I cut Tim off before they could get into a proper fight.

"I'm sorry, Beryl, Tim, but that debate has nothing to do with Diana's murder. I'm more interested in the woman herself, and so will Paddy be when he gets here. If you could leave that until we're through, I'd be grateful."

I allowed them a moment to calm down and lapsed into my confused thoughts.

How did a working class girl from industrial West Yorkshire make it to the stage of La Scala. Well, according to Tim, it was obvious how she did it. She spent much of her time horizontal. But I was puzzled by the initial impetus.

"Tim, did Diana ever tell you how she became interested in opera? I mean, most girls her age would be more interested in Take That or Madonna, or even Taylor Swift."

He shrugged. "Something to do with her dad. He was only a factory worker, but he was fanatical about opera. That's as much as I know."

It was an irrelevance, really. Like asking how come Dennis was an automobile fanatic. Well, I knew why Dennis was an automobile fanatic. Like

Diana, he got it from his father who used to spend his spare time tinkering with cars.

As a distraction, my question did serve its purpose. Whatever was wrong with what Tim had told us, clicked into place in my head.

"Why did you leave the Nooney studios, Tim?"

"Hobson's choice and it was about money," he admitted. "They were going under, largely thanks to Diana Delancey, but I was worth more than they were paying. They couldn't afford it, I got an offer, so I called it day."

It was similar to the tale the Nooneys told us, with one large exception. "Keith Nooney mentioned their financial troubles but he didn't say anything about Diana."

"Yeah, well, see, Diana never paid them for the sessions, cos she said the finished product was inferior. It wasn't. I was the soundman and I tell you there was nothing wrong with those tracks. She was just ducking out of paying for it. Cost the Nooneys a lot of money. I think they're still in business, but it's by the skin of their teeth. They couldn't match the kind of fees I was worth, so I ducked out. Hell, they didn't even pay me for the four weeks I worked on Diana's recordings."

"Our information is that you went to work for a singer rather than another studio. So was that Diana Delancey?"

If he was at all troubled by the question, which would have made a lie of his insistence that he and Diana called it a draw when he left the Nooneys' employ, he didn't show it. "After the damage she did to the Nooneys? Not likely. Anyway, like I told

138

you, I never saw her again once her sessions at Nooneys were over. Until today that it is."

"Then who were you working for?"

"If you must know, it was Mickey Tayking. Comedian, singer, street artist. You must have heard of him."

I shook my head. If Tim was telling the truth, I had no doubt that Simon or Naomi would know who he was talking about. Or even Olivia, assuming she could get her head round such a bizarre stage name.

"He's quite big in his own way," Tim went on, "and he needed a sound engineer for his live work. Someone who could adjust the balances when he switched from high-speed comedy to singing."

"It didn't last long?"

"A year maybe less. He's a bit of a snapper when he wants, is Mickey, and you might think I'm easy to get on with, but I know how to fight my corner. The equipment needed some replacement bits, he went through the roof at the potential cost, I argued back and he paid me up. Next thing I knew, I was at Radio Haxford. Salaried for once in my life. As you know, their sound man retired early through ill-health or something. To be fair to Mickey, he gave me a good reference."

And with that I couldn't think of anything more to ask of him.

But Beryl could and she didn't hesitate to press him. "There's a small window during which we know Diana must have been murdered. Can you account for your whereabouts during that twenty minute gap?"

"I was in my curtained-off cubby hole, Mrs Reitman. You must know. It was about then when the mics went haywire for the first time."

If Beryl didn't know, I did. I remembered Eric throwing open the curtains and Tim crawling about on the floor to put things right.

"I can vouch for you, Tim." I threw down my pen. "I think that's about it, but do bear in mind that when Paddy Quinn gets here, he may want to talk to you again." I gave him an easy smile. "Thanks for your help."

He half rose but Beryl stayed him. "Just a minute. Christine may be done with you, but I want a few words."

Deciding that it was none of my business, I excused myself and left the dining room. The last I saw, Beryl was giving him a solid piece of her mind.

Coming out of the dining room, I suddenly felt drained of energy. A glance at my watch told me it was getting on for half past eleven, and a couple of naps aside, I'd been on the go since crawling out of bed at just before seven that morning. Time, I decided, to call it a night.

I wandered back into the ballroom and stood for a moment, looking for signs of Eric, but as my eye swept around the room I took in fleeting glimpses of the tables, the guests, and something jarred, but I couldn't work out what.

The decorations glittered, the animatronics performed, the fairy lights flickered, Santa and his elves and reindeer called out their yuletide greetings, the sounds drowned by the cacophony of

Reggie's performance on the turntable. Everything shouted Christmas, and yet, there was something not quite right, something that should be there but wasn't.

The dance floor was half full, gowns, shoes, even shirts glistening in the near-stroboscopic lighting as couples indulged their pre-Christmas hedonism. Some were jiving, others were toe to toe, yet others were wrapped in each other's arms, maybe whispering endearments with the promise of licentious excitement to come. At the same time, others remained at their tables, chatting, laughing and joking, some tapping out the rhythm of the obscure piece of music Reggie was pushing through the speakers – something from the early sixties, I guessed. Before my time, anyway. It was a corporate Christmas party. What else would I expect?

I moved around the room, hugging the wall, making for our assigned table where Olivia sat alone, and as I did so, I came upon a small, glittery print, a nativity scene, complete with baby Jesus in the manger, the shepherds, and the star of Bethlehem leading the three wise men and their gifts. I was the kind of person who kept her religious inclinations to herself, but the scene reminded me of the night Ingrid was born, the tears of joy I shed when I held that little girl for the first time, and in later years, a similar flood of emotion when I first held Bethany.

And that's when it struck me. That's when I realised what was missing. Family, children.

Christmas was a family time, a time when the

adults could watch with unmitigated pleasure as children's eyes sparkled with the magic that was Christmas. Another look around the room sent my spirits down. This was corporate, this was strictly adults only. There were no children, no families – or if there were, they were incomplete. This was an almighty, Christmas booze up, and to add to the attraction, it was a freebie. These people were not here to celebrate, they were here to freeload, get smashed out of their brains at no cost to themselves, and for the singles, get it on with whoever they could when the bar shut.

This was not a Capper Christmas. This went against every principle I stood by. Even when I was a police officer, I never joined in with the festive beer ups. As a teenager, I had my share of drunken interludes, but I never got totally blasted simply because it was that time of year, because I never believed that was the spirit of Christmas.

And with this sad train of thought, I found myself engulfed in a welter of self-pity. Christmas was family. My family were close by. Perhaps within five or six miles, certainly less than ten, but they might just as well be on the other side of the world. Thanks to the weather, thanks to Eric Reitman dragooning me into this charade, thanks to some maniac murdering Diana Delancey, I could not get to them and they could not get to me.

By the time I reached the table and joined Olivia, I was pining for my loved ones. I wanted to hear Bethany's laughter, Naomi's lively chatter, Simon's enthusiasm for his job. I even wanted to hear Dennis complaining that he had a few days divorced from the motor cars he loved so much. I wanted to hear his scathing opinions on stunt driving in action movies. "No way could you get away with that in a Ford Escort" or something of that nature. I wanted to hear his soft snores when he nodded off on the settee on Christmas Night during the Strictly Come Dancing special.

I wanted to be home at the heart of my family.

I was not the only one down and depressed when I sat alongside her, Olivia was obviously sick with worry, and it took some coaxing to get it out of her.

"Tim. Him and Mam have been gone ages and he didn't come back with you. She's telling him to keep away from me. I know it."

For the first time that I could recall, I felt some sympathy for the girl and took her hand. "I think she's just trying to ascertain how serious he is about you, love. She doesn't want to see you hurt."

"She's poking her nose in, is what she's doing. I'm not a child, you know. I know what it's all about."

I should hope so, too, I thought. Aloud, I said, "Your mother loves you, Olivia, and she's like any mother. She'll do whatever she must to protect you."

"Yeah but Tim's not like that, Pristine. He's a good man."

You obviously don't know about him and Diana Delancey. The thought rushed into my head and again I kept my trap shut. "You'll see. They'll be back soon and they'll be the best of friends."

Eric appeared from behind Tim's curtain, and joined us. Right away, he asked after his wife and sound man.

I told him of our interview with Tim, leaving out the more salacious points, and brought him up to speed on Beryl's supposed discussion. I didn't mention Olivia by name, but as I said, "Beryl had things she needed to discuss with Tim," I cast enough glances at her for Eric to get the point, and then, I excused myself. "I'm sorry, Eric, but I'm absolutely exhausted. It's time I was out of here."

"Get a good night's sleep, Chrissy, and we'll see you at breakfast."

With a nod to both, I sidled around the wall towards the exit, just as Tim and Beryl came in. I bid them both a pleasant 'goodnight', received the same from Beryl and a scowl from Tim.

Chapter Fourteen

Dennis would have to be up for half past six on the morning of the 23rd, and it was practically certain that he would be in bed by the time I got back to my room, so I didn't bother ringing him. Instead I waited until quarter past seven the following morning.

He wasn't especially pleased to hear from me. "Make it quick, lass. We've got work to do, me and Geronimo."

"Let it wait," I said. "I'm missing you, Dennis. You and Bethany and Naomi and Simon, and I wish I'd never signed on for this thing."

"I did tell you that before you went. Nowt much you can do about it now, though, is there?" He changed the subject. "The filth haven't got to you yet." It was a statement, not a question and it should have forewarned me, but it didn't. I was still too busy feeling sorry for myself.

"Not that I'm aware. I haven't been out of my room yet. What's the weather situation?"

"Better'n it was yesterday. It stopped snowing before I went to bed at midnight, and the ploughs and gritters'll have been out all night. I reckon old knick-knack paddy-whack will be there afore long. And I'd better get back to it. Ring me later."

I didn't get the chance to say more before he rang off. And he never told me if he was missing me. After glowering at the phone for a moment, I was tempted to ring Paddy Quinn, but I changed my mind and instead luxuriated in the shower for ten minutes, after which I spent a further fifteen minutes applying makeup, lipstick, carefully choosing a bland, white top to go with my jeans, and putting my cardi on and only then did I throw back the blinds, and peer out through windows part covered with ice. It was the exterior of the sealed units that were iced up, and I fancied that some of the heat coming through the radiators must have crossed the divide to help thaw the outer pane.

I looked out onto a thin moorland dawn. The sun would not rise for another half hour, but the early twilight was sufficient for me to see that the snow had, indeed stopped, and I could see a vast expanse of land covered in white. Well, it would be, wouldn't it, considering the snow had hardly eased the day before. I had no idea how deep it was, but looking close to the hotel, at the vehicles parked out front, I could see they were up to their wheel hubs in it. The staff of Christmas Manor would have to do some serious digging if the guests were to get away either today or tomorrow. Even as I thought about them, several people appeared and began spreading sand and salt immediately outside the entrance.

Considering the prospect, I guessed that after the murder of Diana Delancey, most would like to be away ASAP, but there were two stumbling blocks with that idea. First, the weather. I still couldn't see the road leading away from the hotel, nor the moorland road which would get them back to Haxford and civilisation.

The second obstacle was rather more formidable and intransigent: DI Paddy Quinn. A dedicated, determined pain in the bottom, he would not allow anyone to leave this hotel until he and his team had spoken to everyone. Wealth, status, assumed importance would not matter to him. I supposed, in his own way, he was a successful and dedicated police officer, completely without fear or favour, but from another angle, he was an irritant, because the rules he applied to Lyle Noelle's guests would also apply to the Radio Haxford crew... including me. And I didn't want to be here. Not after the way I felt the previous night, the way I still felt. I wanted to be home, with my family, where I would be safe, warm, welcome, enjoying myself.

I looked through the window again and in the distance, I could make out the flickering, yellow lights of a vehicle, and I guessed it would be one of the gritters/ploughs Dennis had mentioned.

Rescue.

I felt like a castaway spotting the shape of ship on the distant horizon. I felt like standing up and waving my arms through the window, shouting, 'Here I am. Come and take me home where I belong'. I didn't, of course. If the snow crew below saw me, I'd garner a reputation I didn't really want.

The gritter was still some distance from us, and behind it I could see more lights: headlights, and the familiar blue flashers on vehicle roofs. The police. Paddy and his crew hurtling in like Superman,

Batman, Robin and Wonder Woman (come on, I needed to slot in a female superheroine) to save us from this spectacular yet disturbingly barren landscape.

The law convoy consisted of a large van – personnel carrier if I was not mistaken – and a couple of patrol cars, then a small, dark van, possibly a private ambulance to take Diana to the mortuary, and behind them was another, slightly larger vehicle, one I was sure I recognised. If I didn't know better, I'd swear it was the wrecker belonging to Haxford Fixers, but it couldn't be. Half an hour ago, Dennis was getting ready to go to work, and he had to pick up Tony 'Geronimo' Wharrier first. No way could he be with the police.

Several hundred yards from the hotel, the plough pushed past the entry lane, then stopped, there was some debate, probably over radios, and the police convoy backed up slowly to let the gritter come back and make the sharp left turn towards Christmas Manor. As he did so, the police vehicles moved beyond the entry lane and the other, as yet unidentified vehicle stayed put.

The plough only came as for forward as the furthest vehicle parked outside, then he began to back off. Once reversed back to the main road, he turned towards the waiting police vehicles and the last vehicle came forward. At that point, I realised it was indeed the wrecker belonging to Haxford Fixers and the man behind the wheel would be Dennis Capper.

At the same time, police officers began to emerge from their vehicles. Heavily swathed

148

against the cold, they followed Dennis's vehicle down the road, and when he stopped, they marched past into the building.

The rotten swine. When I spoke to him on the phone, less than ten minutes ago, he misled me into thinking that he was at home and ready to leave and pick up Tony Wharrier before going on to work, when all the time…

Then it dawned on me that he hadn't asked if the police had got to us. He'd said it. He never mentioned picking up Tony, only that they had work to do. Even so, I could imagine him smirking as he followed the police and the gritter up the hill to Haxmoor.

I would get him for that.

But his presence did beg the question why had he been called in? It wasn't as if there were any cars stuck other than those immediately in front of the hotel, and he wouldn't be needed to tow any police vehicle out of the snow. There were enough hands in those vans and patrol cars to cover that eventuality.

So why?

According to my watch, the time was coming up to eight o'clock and there was no point speculating when I could ask the man himself. Anyway, breakfast was calling to me, shouting, 'Time you were feeding yourself, girl.'

With the feeling that I might have to venture out into the snow, I carried my coat for the journey down to the ground floor, and emerged from the lift to find Paddy Quinn reading the riot act to the reception crew, Simon and Mandy Hiscoe in the background stood with Dennis and Tony Wharrier.

"Stop farting about and get him out here. Now," I heard Paddy rant at the receptionist as I strode across the lobby to join my husband, his workmate, my son and one of my best friends.

"What's up, Mandy?" I asked.

"Paddy wants Lyle Noelle down here and the receptionist is stalling." She laughed. "You know what Paddy's like. I want, I get or I wall you up. End of story."

"He needs to speak to George Reynolds, too," I told her.

"No, he doesn't want Noelle here as a suspect he wants him here because he owns this dump."

Her description of Christmas Manor as a 'dump' shocked me slightly, but then, Mandy had always been cynical of five star hikes.

Somewhere the right side of forty, Mandy was senior CID officer permanently on station in Haxford and had been for a number of years. She came under Quinn's control after he moved to Huddersfield when he was promoted. Mandy was a vivacious blonde, unmarried by choice, and a solid, hard-working detective, with a fine record. She had never made inspector because she didn't want to move from Haxford, and promotion would mean a compulsory move since Haxford wasn't big enough for an inspector.

She gave birth to a healthy baby girl, Darlene, a few months back, and consistently refused to name the father. "I don't need any bloke coming between me and Darlene," she had said, and to be fair, motherhood had done her no harm. True, conversations with her tended to be a bit single point, but other than that, she relished the role of mother.

She was also back at work long before her maternity leave was up.

"I could go crazy staring at the walls and waiting for Darlene to wake up, so my old ma is looking after her." She laughed again. "Besides, I can't leave all these bigwigs to Paddy. If he doesn't clap 'em in irons, he'll send 'em all home in tears."

Leaving Mandy, I stretched up and pecked Simon on the cheek. "Don't forget, you, Naomi, and Bethany at ours on the day."

"Even if I don't forget, Mam, you keep reminding me."

"That's what mothers are for." I turned to Dennis and Tony, and my generous smile faded to a look of determination. "And what are you two doing here?"

"Hoping to scrounge some breakfast," Dennis said as he gazed around the lobby. "I don't think I can afford the prices they'll charge."

"That's not what I'm asking, Dennis. Why are you here? You were trying to trick me into believing you were back in Haxford, yet you were driving up here when I spoke to you on the phone."

"I didn't wanna get your hopes up, lass. When you rang, we were still climbing the hill out of Haxford. And I didn't wanna ring you back when we got to the top of the hill, because the wrecker was all over the road."

"Yes, Dennis, I accept all that. But why are you here anyway?"

At this point, Tony Wharrier intervened. The

same age as Dennis, he and my husband had been workmates for longer than anyone cared to remember, but Tony was less obsessed than Dennis (other than bodywork of vehicles, collecting old postcards, and philately – stamp collecting for those of you who don't know the technical term). He was also all ready to answer questions directly rather than hedging the way Dennis often did. And Dennis didn't deliberately flunk questions. While trying to answer them, he was constantly seeking some comparison with repairing engines. As right now, it didn't always work out.

"The police rang early on, Christine," Tony explained. That was another thing about him. He was more polite than Dennis. He always addressed me by my full name. Never Chrissy, never 'hey up lass'. "They guessed, and quite rightly in my opinion, that access to the hotel would be hampered by all those parked cars outside, and it doesn't matter how good they think they are behind the wheel, they'll struggle to get them out of the snow. If we can get the keys, or get the drivers out there, Dennis and I will hook them to the wrecker, and drag them out."

It made a kind of sense. "Why do you need them shifting?"

"Police vehicles," Dennis said. "They need to get the CSI and forensic vans up to the front of the hotel, and of course they'll need the meat wagon to get the stiff away."

I sighed. "I love your terminology, Dennis." I turned back to Tony. "How are Val and the boys?"

"Fine, thank you, Christine. Course, Craig's

wedding never came off, did it. Once the energy prices went up, they called it off. It may happen next year and I'll make sure you and Dennis get an invite."

"Thank you. Give Val my best when you see her. And now, if you'll all excuse me, it's time I was joining my Radio Haxford colleagues for breakfast."

"Any danger of cadging a bacon butty for us?" Typical Dennis.

"Scrounge it yourself."

I turned to leave them, just in time to find Paddy Quinn, his face a mask of anger, bearing down upon us.

"Couldn't run the proverbial in a brewery," he announced. "Apparently, this Noelle bloke what owns the place, isn't even out of bed yet. Lazy git. Right, Christine, I need to know everything you know."

"Very little, Paddy. But you're going to have to wait. I'm going for breakfast."

"No sweat. So am I. I've ordered someone to get this bone idle twonk out of bed and while we're waiting, Mandy, Dennis, Tony, if you want scran, get it, and the hotel will bill police."

I swear that the offer of free food, particularly at breakfast, would see Dennis break the world record for the 100 metres. A split second after Paddy finished speaking, Dennis was already on his way through the dining room doors, and Tony Wharrier wasn't far behind him.

The rest of us followed, but before queuing up for food, I visited my colleagues at their table and told them I would be with the police.

"And they may need to speak to you, Beryl, to confirm some of the things I tell them," I concluded.

She gave me an encouraging smile. "You know where to find me, Christine."

From there I queued up for food: bowl of cereal with skimmed milk and two rounds of toast and marmalade, and as I joined the police, close to the door, Dennis shifted his empty plate, and joined the queue for seconds.

Paddy watched him make his way to the servery. "That husband of yours has just finished a full English, Chrissy, and he's going back to get another plateful?"

"Why do you think I have to carry on working, Paddy? Dennis costs a fortune to feed."

"All right. Business, people. Chrissy, while we eat, tell us what you've learned so far."

I gave him a full rundown, promising to return to my room and collect my notebook after breakfast, and reassuring him that Beryl Reitman was with me throughout the minor work I'd done the previous evening, and she would witness the accuracy of my reports.

"The girl who found the dead woman?"

"Velda Grimes. Lester's daughter. Dennis knows her as does Tony. I'm certain she didn't kill Diana Delancey, but I did warn her that you would need to speak to her."

"I'll leave that one to you, Mandy. Now what's this about this Noelle character and his pal Reynolds?

154

"Arrogant, the pair of them. The type who believe they don't owe anyone any kind of explanation for anything. But I saw them arguing with Diana not long before she died, and neither of them would give us a satisfactory explanation of the cause of that argument."

"They'll answer me or I'll sling both of them in a cell until they learn some manners."

Paddy paused to take a few mouthfuls of bacon and egg. He was about to go on, probably about to detail various duties between Mandy and Simon, when the door flew open and a young woman from reception came in her face white as my clean bed linen.

"It's Mr Noelle," she gasped at Paddy. "He's dead."

Chapter Fifteen

Say what you will about Paddy Quinn and his failings, but indecisiveness was not one of them. The moment the receptionist made the announcement, he was on the radio, calling for uniforms to come into the building.

I was stunned into silence, and even Dennis, who had rejoined us by this time, paused in the middle of eating his second breakfast to gape at the young woman.

When he had done giving out orders, Paddy leapt at his feet, and I rose too. "No way, Chrissy. You're a civilian again now. You wait here. Mandy, hold the fort, Simon, with me."

He and my son disappeared through the door, and I felt some of the depression of the previous evening closing in on me again. In the space of twelve hours, Christmas Manor had become death-row. Back when Eric first told me of the place, I was never fully content with the name Christmas Manor, but now it was even more incongruent. Maybe Lyle Noelle should have looked at horror movies to name his hotel, rather than family entertainment.

And as far as I was concerned, there was only one suspect. George Reynolds. When I said so,

Mandy added a note of caution.

"You should know better than that, Chrissy. I mean, do you have any grounds for accusing this Reynolds character?"

I told her of the argument I'd seen the night before between Noelle, Reynolds and Diana Delancey.

"When he intervened, Lyle Noelle went to town on both Reynolds and Diana, and when we interviewed them later, both were obstructive to say the least. The way I see it, Mandy, Reynolds had a large amount of money invested in this place. Not a problem, you might think, but once Diana Delancey was murdered, you have to wonder how much that would tar the Manor's reputation. If Reynolds was suddenly worried about recouping his investment, he may have gone to see Noelle in the early hours. From there, it wouldn't stretch the imagination much to see an argument developing, and from all I could judge, Reynolds was much fitter, possibly stronger than Noelle."

She pursed her lips and nodded. "I'll bear it in mind, but I'll let you tell Paddy." Her phone warbled for attention. She made the connection and after listening, she looked to Dennis. "What's Grimy doing here?"

Still working his way through the second breakfast, Dennis shrugged and Tony took up the explanation. "He's supposed to be back at the workshop with Greg."

I raised an eyebrow at Mandy. "Vic Hillman," she said with a nod at the phone. "Lester Grimes is outside demanding to be let in."

I understood right away. "Velda, his daughter, must have talked to him either last night or this morning, and we could do with letting him in if only to calm her down."

Mandy gave the proposition a little thought before agreeing. "All right, but that's all. I don't want him poking his nose in anywhere else, and if I catch him nicking anything…" She trailed off.

I stood again. "I'll handle it if you like, Mandy."

She chuckled. That was more like Mandy. "And deal with Vic Hillman?"

I put my coat on, ready to brave the weather. "The day I can't put Minx in his place, is the day I give up."

The coat was a good idea. Well, it would be, wouldn't it, considering the landscape, bathed in strong, December sunlight, looked like a polar icecap. The moment I left the warm cocoon of the building I got a sense of that old music hall joke. I don't know where the wind was coming from but I knew where it was going, and I was glad I wore my jeans and not a skirt.

Immediately outside the front entrance, the considerable bulk of Sergeant Vic Hillman barred Lester Grimes's way into the hotel. Beyond the pair I could see the CSI team disposing of their winter topcoats and pulling on their forensic suits and overshoes. Diana Delancey's body had had about twelve hours in a warm-ish environment; time enough for it to get a little high. Whether they'd been made aware of Lyle Noelle's demise, I had no idea, and right at that moment, it wasn't an issue. Hillman and Grimy were.

Vic was already a serving officer when I signed on, and we had never been slow to irritate each other. At some point, Dennis mentioned Hillman motorcars, specifically the Imp and the Minx. Considering Hillman stood something like six feet six, I didn't see the point of calling him an Imp, so I christened him Minx. (You should have realised by now that Haxford was a town that enjoyed indulging in nicknames, hence my own Capper the Copper, Dennis's Cappy, Tony Wharrier's Geronimo, and so on.) From the word Go, Hillman detested his nickname, but it stuck, and he was noticeably short with anyone who used it to his face.

Not that Hillman's annoyance troubled Lester. Short, unkempt, living up to *his* nickname, Grimy, he was one of the junior partners at Haxford Fixers, an electrician by trade, and had dabbled with household appliances and automobile electrics. He was noticeably fond of Haxford Best Bitter, usually to excess, and his only other fix was warbling on the karaoke in the Engine House pub (nickname, the Sump Hole). Of the three founders of Haxford Fixers, he was far and away the laziest. Dennis and Tony earned more for the simple reason that they put in more effort. Lester's love of too much drink had cost him two marriages, one of them being Velda's mother, and garnered a reputation as a self-employed, neo-alcoholic layabout. But it wasn't often you could see him in a fit of temper as he was now.

"Listen, Minx, my little girl's in there, and she was crying her eyes out on the phone. She needs her

159

dad."

"Call me Minx again, and she will be able to see her dad in the nick. Now clear off before I lock you up."

"On what charge?"

"It's a crime scene, dipstick. You can't go in there. Now—"

"Excuse me, Vic," I interrupted. "Mandy has just authorised him to go in."

Hillman turned on me, his face a mask of suspicion. "Well, she never said nowt to me."

"Lester's daughter is distressed, and she still has to face Paddy. I've talked it over with Mandy, and we believe that if she could see her dad, it'll help calm her down for when they come to take a statement."

Hillman took out his phone. "Wait there."

In an effort to prove just how awkward he could be, he rang Paddy, who, of course, knew nothing about Lester's arrival nor the debate between Mandy and me. I couldn't hear what Paddy said, but it was a crystal clear rant, at the end of which Hillman apologised for disturbing him, cut the call, and then called Mandy.

A minute later, he ended the call again, and glared first at me, then at Lester. "You can go in but you, Grimy, keep your light fingers to yourself."

"Bog off... Minx."

I led the way into the hotel, and as I unbuttoned my coat, Lester removed his, revealing a shabby shirt that looked as if it hadn't seen the inside of a washing machine since Hotpoint did away with twin tubs.

160

As we crossed the lobby, a thought occurred to me, and I put aside my feelings about his crumpled, ragged attire. "How did you get here, Lester?"

It was a valid question. He'd been banned from driving some years previously and had to choose between wheels and drink. Drink won, and he let his licence go.

"I bagged a lift off Rocky."

My mind filled with visions of Sly Stallone. What was he doing here in Haxford? "Rocky?"

"Billy Rockliffe. You know him. He drives one of the gritters for the council. The ploughs came up first, then the filth, then your Dennis, and Rocky was right at the back of the queue, gritting and salting the road so everyone can get back down when they're finished. Our Velda rang me at half past ten last night and told me what was going on. Well, I was a bit tanked up because I was dossing in the Sump Hole, but her mam, Marge, rang me at six this morning and told me to get my backside in gear and get up here to sort the girl out, and I guessed that Rocky would be on call, so I bummed a lift off him." He stopped, gripped my arm and gently turned me to face him. "Tell me she's not in any trouble, Chrissy."

In all the years I had known Lester Grimes, I had never seen him this concerned over anyone, and it was a lesson to me. In most people's opinion, Lester Grimes's only concern was Lester Grimes. This proved popular opinion to be wrong.

"She is very upset, Lester. Or at least she was when I saw and spoke to her last night. She found the body, slipped in the blood – which she thought

161

was wine - and when she came to me, Velda was covered in blood, but I'm certain that she didn't kill the poor woman."

He shook his head. "Nah, no way would she hurt anyone. But I suppose Paddy Quinn's ready for charging her, is he?"

"If he does, he'll have me to reckon with. Come on. Let's see if we can get you a cup of tea."

Did I really say 'a cup of tea'? Lester helped himself to a full English breakfast, and two cups of tea, which he carried back to the table.

"Snooty so and so's," he said when he joined us. "Asked me what I was doing dressed like this."

"So what did you tell them?" Mandy asked.

Diving into a large piece of sausage, dipped in egg yolk, Lester said, "I told him I was the body man working for the cops, and I was only waiting on the stiffs so I could go on my way." He swallowed the mouthful. "By the way, I told them to charge it to the police."

Even Mandy was forced to smile.

Dennis had other things on his mind. "If you're here, Grimy, who's minding the shop?"

"Good Boy."

Mandy frowned. "Who's Good Boy?"

"Greg Vetch," Dennis explained. "You see, I'm Cappy, Geronimo's Geronimo, Grimy's Grimy, and when Good Boy joined us we had to think of a name for him, and we couldn't. But his name sounds like 'fetch' and when you throw a stick for a dog and it brings it back, you pat the dog on the head and say, good boy. So he became Good Boy."

"I never subscribed to it," Tony Wharrier told

me.

"Well, it's better than sausage roll," Lester said between mouthfuls of bacon and fried tomatoes. Looking around the table, he explained, "Gregg's sell sausage rolls."

I was still marvelling at the untapped creativity of everyday Haxforders when Paddy turned up, his face as black as the Haxford sky in a summer thunderstorm. One glance at Lester, polishing his plate with dry bread, was enough to set the inspector off.

"What is he doing here?"

"Supporting his daughter," Mandy said. "According to Chrissy, Velda was very distressed, and without someone here to calm her down, we won't get much sense out of her."

"Well, I hope he's paid for that breakfast."

"He has," I put in. "Did you get the message from Mandy about George Reynolds?"

"Why do you think I'm so steamed up? Yes, I got the message, and yes, we went along to Reynolds's room, and he's not there. When I checked at reception just now, they told me his car's gone too."

Dennis, who was on his fourth cup of tea or thereabouts, disagreed. "No way has he got away from this place."

"Then where's his car?"

"As if I'd know, but there's only one road away from this place, and we came up that way. He didn't pass us, and I don't believe he could have got down there during the night. If he tried to leg it from here, he must have been suicidal."

"He could have gone the other way," Paddy said. "Towards Longendale."

Dennis still would not have it. "The road's still shut."

"We don't know that. Besides, he could have driven on top of the snow. He was running a 4x4."

Dennis shrugged. "And how do you reckon he would have got down the other side? The gradient's about one in six. You reckon he's sledged his way down, do you?"

Paddy was on the point of explosion. "So what do you think, Dennis?"

"If he tried to run for it, then ten to one he came off the road somewhere, and the best thing you can do, is get a chopper up to check the areas just off the road. If I'm right, his car will be covered in ice by now, and it'll be practically invisible from the road. Anyway, for all we know, he might have left while it was still snowing."

Paddy was appalled. "A chopper? That'll cost a fortune, and we do have budgets you know."

My husband shrugged. "In that case, you'll have to wait while it thaws."

At this point, I intervened. "Just a minute, Paddy. What's so urgent about speaking to George Reynolds? I mean, when I put the point to Mandy, it was based on nothing more than an argument last night which neither man explained properly."

"Yes, well, based on your observations, it was either Noelle or Reynolds in the frame for murdering this woman. Noelle has been killed in exactly the same way. Knife in the throat. Blood everywhere. CSI will be in there for the rest of the day, and probably tomorrow. Work it out for yourself, Chrissy. Two people dead, and according to you Reynolds argued with them both, and Reynolds has done a bunk. It's him. I guarantee it."

Chapter Sixteen

The day would be one of the most tedious and wearisome that I could recall. The police took routine statements from everyone, a more detailed account from Beryl and Eric Reitman, and of course, me. They interviewed Velda, took her clothing for forensic analysis, but even Paddy maintained that she was not guilty. It was merely a case of procedure. After that, she and Lester, who had sat in on her interview, were told they could leave, and the last we saw them, Dennis was pulling Velda's Vauxhall Corsa out of the snow, so that she and her father could go back to Haxford.

Around eleven in the morning everyone was herded into the ballroom and left there while the bodies were removed from their rooms, and taken to the mortuary ambulance. After that, Paddy took to the stage, and told everyone that should they wish to leave, they were at liberty to do so once they had been interviewed, and Dennis and Tony Wharrier were on hand to help any drivers stuck in the snow the way they had helped Velda retrieve her car.

Most of the guests took the police advice, and left the hotel, and between eleven and about half past one, Dennis and Tony were kept busy, towing cars out of the deeper snow so that the owners could be on their way.

By half past two in the afternoon, Dennis and Tony had freed the remaining cars so that if their owners decided to leave, they could, and my husband and his senior partner were ready for calling it a day. I yearned to climb into that wrecking truck and go with them, but I couldn't. When I put the proposition to Eric, he was most insistent.

"You have your Lost Friends slot at seven o'clock, Chrissy. I'm sorry, but you'll have to stay behind and go home with us tomorrow morning."

I gestured around at the half empty ballroom. "Who am I going to be talking to, Eric? If we're lucky, there might be ten people left by the time I'm on, and most of those will be staff."

"I'm not thinking of the live audience," he said. "I'm thinking of the station. You're advertised as coming live from here at seven o'clock. I'm sorry, but we have no choice. Of course, if it's really that bad, we may very well wrap up and go home tonight after your slot. I can't give you anything definite but if we were able to leave by, say, ten-ish, would you be all right with that?"

I wasn't, but I was quite skilled at lying. "It would be better than spending another night in this chamber of horrors."

Matters would not go to plan anyway. At two o'clock Paddy received a call from Haxford police station after a television news station rang in with a report. One of their helicopters was overflying the moors checking out the snow when the pilot spotted a car run off the road and rolled over into a ditch.

Dennis and Tony were just about to drive away, when Paddy stopped them, and presently a small convoy, one plough and several police vehicles followed by Dennis made its way back along the road towards Haxford, leaving the Radio Haxford team, Mandy and me waiting for more news.

Dennis, I knew, would be loving it. Whenever he worked for the police, he charged by the hour and I had a feeling that his rate for the wrecker was about fifty pounds per hour. The clock began ticking the moment he left Haxford Fixers' premises and it didn't stop until he got back there. He must have been on the road for seven that morning, from our house in this case, and he would be unlikely to get back much before half past five or six o'clock. Knowing my husband, he would round up to the next hour, so if he got back at ten past six, he would charge the police until seven o'clock. Greedy? Yes, and he was quite unrepentant. "If they want the best, they have to pay for it," he always insisted.

But that worked on the arbitrary assumption that he was the best. I wouldn't argue with his self-assessment, but only because I didn't know enough about the business.

During the interim, Harry and Yolande Kneale took the stage, and belted out a range of Carpenters' numbers to a ballroom that was all but empty except for a clutch of police officers and a few hotel staff. Even though I had to put on a similar, pointless performance later in the evening, I felt sorry for them. It was as if they were street musicians, playing for all they were worth, but ignored by the passers-by. In this instance, they weren't ignored because there were no passers-by to ignore them.

Their set lasted a little over forty-five minutes, and the moment they were done, they began to dismantle their minimal equipment (electronic keyboard, guitar, amps, mics etc.).

"The minute these people pay us, we're out of here," Harry told me when I got chatting to them.

"Have you far to go?"

"Manchester. Technically, it's about fifteen miles from here, but thanks to this flaming snow, we'll have to double back to Haxford, then Huddersfield, pick up the M62, and even then it's about another twenty miles home."

Once again, I felt sorry for them but I wished them well as they packed up and made ready to leave.

We and the police were about the only people left in the ballroom when Eric called for sound balance checks. "The weather sent the equipment crazy last night, so we need to check that everything is in working order now."

Tim, who had been sat with us most of the afternoon, got to his feet, and hobbled off towards his cubbyhole.

"Have you hurt yourself?" I asked.

He gave me a wry grin. "Last night. Slipped in the snow, didn't I? Knocked my ankle, and hurt my elbow. Good job I was wearing a pair of stout boots and a thick coat, or I could have come away with a couple of broken bones."

As he wandered off, Olivia giggled. "He was gone for ages and absolutely freezing when he came back to the room."

That puzzled me. "What was he doing?"

"Not sure, Justine. He went out to the bus for something. Must have been something he forgot. Took him ages to find it."

"But surely…"

I shut up as sound began to come through the speakers, and we lost the next three quarters of an hour in a repeat of the previous day's tests, including me having to read from a non-existent prompt while Eric, Reggie, Beryl, Olivia, and me when I wasn't rabbiting, checked the balances from all corners of the room.

Shortly after, with the clock getting on for half past four, while I puzzled on the things I had heard, the wrecker, now carrying the half-crushed remains of what had been a glitzy, nearly new Range Rover, got back to the hotel and the police vans were right behind it.

A few minutes later, Paddy came in wearing a face like a wet weekend in Withernsea. To be more accurate it was more like a black blizzard in Bognor. I've never actually been to Bognor but it was the only seaside resort I could think of which begins with the letter B… other than Bridlington, but I like Bridlington.

In an effort to soothe his obvious angst, I asked, "Does the car belong to Reynolds, Paddy?"

"Yes, and he's flaming well in it, isn't he?"

"Oh dear. And did he freeze to death or was he killed when the vehicle rolled over?"

"Neither. It looks like he was stabbed in the neck just like Noelle and the Delancey woman. We won't know for sure until the fire brigade get here with a can opener and get the roof off. That's why your Dennis had to bring him back here. We can't work out on the moor. It's colder than a polar bear's—"

"I think we get the picture," I interrupted.

"Yes, well, at least we get a bit of shelter from the buildings here." He fumed for a moment. "What we have to do now is work out when he and his killer drove out of here. Whoever it was, Reynolds wasn't driving. He's in the passenger seat. We need the CCTV for this place."

Mandy left her seat. "Get a brew or something, Paddy. I'll speak to reception."

She disappeared, Paddy signalled for a waiter and ordered himself a cup of coffee, and as it was delivered, Dennis and Tony Wharrier came in, looked around, spotted us, and made a beeline for our table.

Both were wearing heavy topcoats. Tony supplemented his with a woolly hat in Huddersfield Town's blue and white, while Dennis sported a Trapper's hat, complete with ear muffs, covering his head and ears and strapped beneath his chin.

"How long are we gonna be, Paddy?" Dennis asked as they sat with us. "Only this is costing you a pretty penny."

"The police service, Dennis, not me. I'm sorry, I don't know. We're waiting for the Fire Brigade. I need Reynolds's body out of that Range Rover ASAP, and the doc's on station here with the rest of us."

Tony collared Paddy's waiter, ordered tea for himself and Dennis, and took up the debate. "Dennis and I were talking, and we could get the wreck down to the fire station if that's easier. All we need is one of the gritters crawling down the hill in front of us, just to make sure they're dealing with the ice on the road."

Paddy gave the idea of a moment's consideration, took out his phone and made the call. A minute or two later, he shut the phone down, and spoke to my husband and his workmate. "You're on. You can get on your way now."

"Aye, well, we'll just have a cuppa, first," Dennis said. "I wonder if there's any danger of a butty to go with it."

Typical Dennis. When he wasn't feeding the bottomless pit that was his stomach, he was thinking about feeding it.

"Wait until you get home, Dennis," I said.

He turned his attention to me. "What about you? Seems as if everyone else has gone home, so do you want to come with me and Geronimo?"

I shook my head as Mandy came back into the room. "I can't. I have to deliver Lost Friends from here. But Eric did say we might be on our way home later tonight rather than tomorrow."

Beryl gestured towards her husband whose phone was glued to his ear. "Eric's talking to the studio now, seeing what he can arrange." She waved around the near empty ballroom. "No one here to listen to you, Chrissy."

Mandy rejoined us and derailed the discussion with more bad news. "Sorry, boss, but the CCTV went down last night. They're waiting for an engineer to come and mend it, but chances are, he won't get here this side of Christmas."

172

It did not do Paddy's mood any favours. "Damn and blast. What time did it shut down? I mean, was it still running early enough for us to catch whoever drove away with Reynolds?"

"No such luck. It went down about quarter to eleven last night."

Olivia, whose face indicated that she had been drifting through an interstellar void, better known as her mind, was suddenly alert. "It was the weather," she said. "They made Mrs Clapper's microphones go crackers at the same time."

And with that simple announcement from a young woman I considered a simpleton, I had more than an inkling of what had been going on. I opened my mouth to speak, but before I could say a word, Eric was at our side.

"Chrissy, I've just spoken to the boss in Haxford, and he's agreed to let us record now. Although the show's billed as going out live, there's no one here to listen to you, so we might as well get it done. They'll add an applause track on it down in the studio, and they'll broadcast at seven as planned. Once we got this thing in the can, say forty-five minutes, we can start packing up the trailer and making our way home."

"Does Oscar need a tow with the trailer? You know. Get it out of the snow?" Dennis asked as I made my way to the stage, my mind only half on the recording of Lost Friends.

I didn't hear Eric's response, but as I took my seat, our driver, Oscar, now in the ballroom, was discussing the situation with my husband.

The audience, as Eric said, was minimal, and I

173

was so familiar with Lost friends, that reading the prompts was second nature to me. We usually did two broadcasts a week, which came to an hour of broadcast time (including commercial and music breaks) but in actual fact was only about forty minutes of recording time. Ignoring the small audience of police and hotel staff, I read out the list of people and the lost friends/relatives they were trying to get in touch with, adding the occasional pause, introducing the odd piece of music as per the script and leaving a gap after it so the music could be fitted in. It was the standard process but this time it was happening in this grand ballroom rather than my conservatory.

By a quarter to six, Eric professed himself happy with the recording. It was a miracle considering that my concentration was less on Lost Friends, more focused on the murders of Diana Delancey, Lyle Noelle, and George Reynolds.

I stepped from the stage and technicians moved in to begin dismantling the equipment. Leaving them to it, I first made my way outside where Dennis, Tony and Oscar were making an effort to turn our bus round. I had a quick word with Oscar, which amounted to one question and a simple answer, then I returned to our table in the ballroom, where I kept my voice down as I leaned in to speak to Paddy and Mandy.

"I know what's been going on. I know who did it. And if you can get him to the dining room, I promise you, we'll close the case tonight."

Chapter Seventeen

When they brought Tim in, I was sat with Mandy and Paddy, and in deference to me (hopefully) getting all the right answers, they let me start proceedings.

I kept my voice as civil as I could. "I know it was you, Tim, but there are some gaps I haven't been able to fill in."

He made some pretence at remaining calm. "What was me?"

"You murdered Diana Delancey, Lyle Noelle, and George Reynolds. I know you did."

"Twaddle. I did nothing of the kind."

"Oh but you did. You see, you were too sure of yourself, and of course, you relied on the worst alibi you could. Olivia Reitman. You assumed that she's plain thick; stupid. And that's not the case. Trouble is, she takes everything at face value, so when you told her you went out to the bus last night, she accepted that, but it never occurred to you that she would tell me and her mother the same story. When I spoke to Oscar, our driver, I learned that he keeps the bus and the trailer locked up and I knew you'd lied. So what were you really doing outside?" I leaned forward to hammer home my point. "Cutting the camera feeds for the hotel's CCTV, that's

175

what."

He laughed and directed his question at Paddy. "Are you taking this drivel seriously?"

Paddy did not answer. Instead, I did.

"When we worked the timings out, the cameras went down at precisely the same time as the microphones and lighting went haywire for the second time. Just as I was coming to the end of my account of the Graveyard Poisoner. You told Eric you had to answer a call of nature, and I saw you sneaking out and then back down the far side of the ballroom back to your corner. At least, I thought you were sneaking. In fact, you were limping. But you weren't limping earlier when Beryl and I talked to you. I think the ladder slipped as you were coming down after cutting the CCTV feed. Am I right? That's how you hurt your leg and your elbow. But cutting that camera feed was vital, because you couldn't afford to have anyone see you driving George Reynolds out of here in the early hours."

Despite his best efforts to hide it, I could see the concern coming to his eyes, and I pressed home my advantage.

"The only thing I can't work out is how you got to Diana, but I have a theory. I just about noticed you leave for your alleged visit to the toilets when I was on stage, but I imagine most of the audience didn't because they were concentrating on me. The same probably goes for earlier in the evening, the time when Diana was killed. I saw you crawling around the floor of your curtained-off corner, but for all I know, you could have slinked out and back in without anyone noticing. Not even me, and you

176

had to pass me both ways."

"You're talking out of your—"

Paddy interrupted. "Forensics will go through Reynolds's car like a curry going through a dog with diarrhoea. It doesn't matter how careful you think you've been, Farrell, we'll find traces of you, and when we do, you're sunk. Better to tell us it all right now."

Tim sat fuming for a long moment. I guess he was trying to find some way of wriggling out of it, but when he spoke, I was wrong... and not only about that.

He pointed an accusing finger at me. "She's as big an idiot as Olivia. You've got it wrong, Miss Marbles. I didn't kill Diana. As far as I was concerned, she owed me a lot of money. The money the Nooneys couldn't pay me because she wouldn't pay them. When I collared her at the sound tests yesterday, I was demanding the cash, and she told me right where I could go but I warned her I wasn't going to back off. I wanted what I was due."

"And you lost your temper and killed her," Mandy said.

"Wrong. It was Reynolds who killed her. She'd threatened to expose the way he used her when he was giving her a leg up in the early days. And we all know what I mean by 'used her'. That was the argument between them you saw at the ballroom door. Noelle told them both to can it, but he was buddy-buddy with Reynolds, and as we all know, Reynolds sank a shedload of money into this dump. If he was going to come down on anyone's side, it would be Reynolds's. Noelle knew what Diana was

177

like, so he threatened to expose her habit of sleeping her way to the top. Noelle followed her out of the ballroom, yes, but he went back to his office. Reynolds didn't. He trailed her to the ladies and shut her up for good."

This came as a surprise, but I wasn't beaten yet. "Let me get this straight. You knew about Reynolds abuse of her in advance, didn't you?"

He nodded. "Diana told me about it during the month she and I were... you know. And she told me she would get him back one day. When she was killed last night, I knew it was either Reynolds or Noelle. I cornered Noelle in his room at two this morning, and he coughed the lot. He was ready to ruin Diana and back Reynolds, and he knew that Reynolds had knifed her." He was gradually getting angrier. "She was dead, I had no chance of getting the ten grand I was due, and I knew he'd warn Reynolds about me, so I knifed him. Payback as far as I was concerned. Then I picked up Georgie boy from his room, and took him down to his car at knifepoint. And before you ask, no one saw us because we left through the kitchen door." Tim laughed. "You never saw a guy so scared. And when I told him why I was so mad, he offered to pay me whatever I'd lost thanks to Diana plus a few grand to keep my mouth shut. I didn't trust him, so I made him drive along the road for half a mile, then forced him into the passenger seat. That's when I cut him. Then I drove a bit further, aimed the car at the ditch, and jumped out, and that, Mrs Smarty Pants, is when I hurt myself. Not falling off the flaming ladder. See? When I sneaked back into the ballroom, I really was sneaking, not limping."

I swallowed some of my pride. "But you did cut the camera, didn't you?"

"Of course I did. I didn't want anyone see us getting into Reynolds's Range Rover."

"And you did make the electrics go haywire."

"The second time yes. The first time it really was the weather. I'm an expert, remember. It's my job. Loosen a jack and the general vibrations running through the ballroom was enough to do the rest."

"And you did sneak out without anyone noticing you... except me, that is."

"I just told you, I sneaked back in, so yes, I sneaked out, too. Easy-peasy. Everyone in the place was riveted on you and your stupid stories." He became less proud of his expertise, more forceful in his reasoning. "She owed me about ten k, and I figure I could persuade her to pay. Reynolds and to some degree Noelle took that away from me. As far as I'm concerned, they got what they deserved."

I shook my head. "And that's where we disagree, Tim. Reynolds should have paid for what he did, yes, but not with his life, and I really can't see what Lyle Noelle did wrong."

"He knew too much and he'd have helped get Reynolds off the hook."

"Well, we'll never know now, will we?" I got to my feet. "I'll leave you to deal with him, Paddy."

***

Olivia was inconsolable when Beryl and I took her to one side and told her.

179

Through floods of tears, she cursed him. "He's just been using me, hasn't he, Justine? Making sure he gets what he wants. He doesn't care about me."

I took her hand. For all her simplistic view of the world, she still had her feelings and they were hurt. I felt really sorry for her. "I don't think that's true, Olivia. I think he genuinely cared about you, but he was an angry man. A man who'd been cheated out of thousands of pounds."

"But he had a job, he was earning a wage, and we'd have been all right because I was working as well."

I think Beryl was secretly glad that Tim had been exposed as a killer and was on his way to prison, but she refrained from saying so and hugged her daughter. That's what mothers do. Right, wrong, stupid, it didn't matter. A mother would defend her sons and daughters no matter what they were, what they'd done... even if it meant burying their own feelings towards those who hurt their children.

"I'm sure Tim didn't mean it to come to this, love," Beryl said. "You'll get over it. And there are plenty of young men out there who'll take a shine to a lovely woman like you. Aren't there, Chrissy?"

"At your age, Olivia, the world is your playground, and you can take your pick of men." *But improve your aim next time.* The thought leapt into my head but I kept it to myself.

We eventually calmed her down and set about packing for home.

I don't know how Dennis, Tony, and Oscar managed it, but when we eventually left the hotel at just after eight o'clock, the bus was facing the right way with the trailer hooked on, the engine running, the heaters warmed up, and we were ready for the off.

The journey back to Haxford was as big a nightmare as the outbound, but we were in convoy with Dennis and Tony, still carrying George Reynolds's crumpled Range Rover, ahead of us, most of the police vehicles behind, and a gritter leading the way. I estimated our speed down that hill at about five mph. and considering the icy conditions, it was fast enough for me.

I've lived in Haxford all my life, but I don't ever recall a time when I was so pleased to see my home turf. Rather than dropping me off at home, which would be another toil for Oscar and his bus and trailer, I left with everyone else outside the market hall, and got a taxi to take me home.

I was there before Dennis and the house was freezing. First job was to switch on the central heating, and then check on my darling Cappy the Cat. I had been gone two days, and he didn't give a fig. He blatantly ignored me, as if castigating me for having gone away and left him to Hazel McQuarrie's tender mercies. He soon changed his mind when I put a feed down for him.

Eventually, with the fire throwing out heat from the hearth and the central heating coming up to working temperature, I settled down with a cup of tea, and reflected on the weekend.

For a wannabe radio personality, it wasn't the best of starts. The shocking weather, the innate snobbery of some of the people I'd encountered, and of course the grim death toll, had yielded a baptism of fire rather than a gentle introduction to the full-time world of radio.

Dennis, still driving the wrecker, albeit minus George Reynolds's wrecked Range Rover, got home just before ten, and he was wagging his tail like the friendly dog we didn't own.

"Hey up, lass, do you know how much we've made today, working for the filth? Me and Geronimo? A flaming fortune. I bet Paddy'll have some explaining to do when his bosses see the bill."

"Good for you, Dennis."

My mood struck him right away. "Fed up?"

"Glad to be home, if I'm to tell the truth. It's been an absolute nightmare."

"Well, I did warn you."

"So you did. And now it's time for me to warn you. Tomorrow is Christmas Eve and we have a load of shopping to do."

"Aw, Chrissy—"

I cut him off. "You'll be finishing at lunchtime because you always do, and you'll meet me in the market hall, and don't turn up in that wrecker. Be ready to load the shopping into your car and mine and you'll be helping me sort it out when we get home." I sighed and stared at the glow of the coal-effect fire. "It's Christmas, and I intend enjoying it with my family."

Epilogue

Christmas came and went, New Year followed, and as a family we threw ourselves into it with the same fervour we always did. A party at our place on the day, a visit to Simon and Naomi on Boxing Day, Dennis put in a few hours at Haxford Fixers over the interim, and on New Year's Eve, Tony and Val Wharrier invited us to a massive party at their place, which went on until the early hours of the morning. Neither Dennis nor I saw the light of day until gone noon on New Year's Day.

With the start of the year, my commitments to Radio Haxford aside, my diary was free, and I passed the time doing nothing more exciting than mooch around the house, but it gave me the space I needed to contemplate the events at Christmas Manor and the effect they had on me.

Although it was a nightmare best confined to the kind of memories I would rather be without, I took some satisfaction from identifying Tim Farrell as the major miscreant, and that very fact made me question my decision to rescind my part-time career as a private investigator.

At our meeting in Terry's Tea Bar back on December 6th, Eric had insisted that once I signed a contract with Radio Haxford, I would have to give up my work as a private eye so as to ensure that I was always free to record my programs. And yet, if Christmas Manor demonstrated anything it was that I was a skilled investigator, less hasty than Paddy Quinn, but just as capable of arriving at the correct conclusion.

Listener feedback on Christine Capper's Mystery Hour was phenomenal. It drew one of the largest audiences Radio Haxford had ever enjoyed, but it didn't enjoy universal approval. There was a slight majority in favour, many of them demanding more of the same. I was a (qualified) success.

Could I legitimately knit together my embryonic career in radio with my experience as a private detective, and avoid upsetting Eric or my clients? It was a dilemma almost as troubling as the one I suffered during the Leach case. But by January 3rd, I had made my decision.

Yes, Christine Capper would become one of the new voices of Radio Haxford, yes, she would carry on delivering her vlog every Thursday, but no matter what complications it created, she would also remain Haxford's only licensed private investigator.

THE END

THANK YOU FOR READING. I HOPE YOU HAVE ENJOYED THIS BOOK. WOULD YOU BE KIND ENOUGH TO LEAVE A RATING OR REVIEW ON AMAZON?

The Author

David W Robinson retired from the rat race after the other rats objected to his participation, and he now lives with his long-suffering wife in sight of the Pennine Moors outside Manchester.

Best known as the creator of the light-hearted and ever-popular **Sanford 3rd Age Club Mysteries**, and in the same vein, **Mrs Capper's Casebook**. He also produces darker, more psychological crime thrillers as in the **Feyer & Drake** thrillers and occasional standalone titles.

He, produces his own videos, and can frequently be heard grumbling against the world on Facebook at https://www.facebook.com/davidrobinsonwriter/ and has a YouTube channel at https://www.youtube.com/user/Dwrob96/videos. For more information you can track him down at www.dwrob.com and if you want to sign up to my newsletter and pick up a #FREE book or two, you can find all the details at https://dwrob.com/readers-club/

By the same Author
Mrs Capper's Casebook

Christine Capper is a solid, down to earth Yorkshire lass, witty, plain spoken, but with an innate sense of inquiry (all right, then, she's nosy). She passes her days in the West Yorkshire town of Haxford looking after her long-suffering husband, Dennis, a man with an obsession for all things automotive, and putting him right when he goes wrong, which is more often than not. She takes care of their pet, Cappy the Cat, a feline with attitude, dotes on her granddaughter Bethany, and is openly proud of her son, Simon, now Acting Detective Constable Capper of the Haxford force.

A former police officer, she's Haxford's only trained and licenced private investigator. She's choosy about the cases she takes on but appears destined to be dragged into more serious affairs, during which she passes on her findings to her friend, Detective Sergeant Mandy Hiscoe and Mandy's immediate boss, DI Paddy Quinn, a man who is quite open about his dislike for private eyes.

A series of light-hearted mysteries, laced with Yorkshire grit and wit, Mrs Capper's Casebooks are exclusive to Amazon available for the Kindle and in paperback.

You can find them at:
https://mybook.to/cappseries

The Sanford 3rd Age Club Mysteries

*These titles are published and managed by
Darkstroke Books*

A decade on from their debut, there are 26 volumes (soon to be 27) and a special in the Sanford 3rd Age Club Mystery series.

We follow the travels and trials of amateur sleuth Joe Murray and his two best friends, Sheila Riley and Brenda Jump. The short, irascible Joe, proprietor of The Lazy Luncheonette in Sanford, West Yorkshire, jollied along by the bubbly Brenda and Sheila, but only his friends, but also his employees, all three leading lights in the Sanford 3rd Age Club (STAC for short). And it seems that wherever they go on their outings on holidays in the company of the born-again teenagers of the 3rd Age Club, they bump into… MURDER.

A major series of whodunits marinated in Yorkshire humour, they are exclusive to Amazon and you can find them at: **https://mybook.to/stac**

Other Works

I also turn out darker works such as The Anagramist and The Frame with Chief Inspector Samantha Feyer and civilian consultant Wesley Drake, and the standalone The Cutter.

For details visit **https://dwrob.com/the-dark/**

Free Books

Like what you've seen so far? Why to subscribe to my newsletter? I guaranteed that you will not be inundated with emails, and your address will never be sold on. Once you sign up, you will receive details of to one but TWO free novellas.

For more information visit
https://dwrob.com/readers-club/

Printed in Great Britain
by Amazon